T0054336

Praise for *The Sitter*

'*The Sitter* is phenomenal. A remarkable feat and enthralling work, *The Sitter* is elegantly constructed – a book that weaves between reality and unreality and wonder with supreme ease. The nested scenes work perfectly, with not a word nor theme nor scene wasted. It moves through layers like music, up and down registers of hope and awe, regret, sadness and self-knowledge. The historical aspects are fascinating, the contemporary scenes compelling. O'Keeffe's work floats. I was utterly spellbound.'

—Michelle Johnston

'Meditative and elegant, *The Sitter* by Angela O'Keeffe is the story of two women who find themselves in the study of each other. Their stories, their connections, are beautifully layered in this touching novel.'

—Mirandi Riwoe

'A gorgeous book, deft, tender, clear-eyed, about seeing and being seen; being and having been. A book that shimmers in the space between writer and reader, so full of life and light and knowledge I had to pause over and again to allow the pleasure of the language and images to settle in me before moving on.'

—Kate Cole-Adams

'In an ingenious reversal, Angela O'Keeffe conjures Paul Cezanne's wife and sitter, Hortense, out of the canvas and on to the page to observe her contemporary Australian writer. Hortense transcends time, language and country to narrate this strange and beautiful hallucination on the endlessly shifting boundary between art and life.'

—**Fiona Kelly McGregor**

'*The Sitter* is a spellbinding work that will challenge readers to let go of their preconceptions of what fiction should be, give in to the undertow, and be carried away … It is an elegant mosaic that interrogates power, female relationships, and the purpose of art.'

—***Books+Publishing***

'Exquisite storytelling.' —***Australian Women's Weekly***

'*The Sitter* is a beautiful surprise of a book and a highlight of my reading year so far.'

—**Alison Huber,** *Readings Monthly*

'… a satisfyingly provocative and elusive piece of writing.'

—***The Age* and *Sydney Morning Herald***

'Compelling and playful … For all of its interest in imagination and art, and in looking and being seen, *The Sitter* is at its heart a novel about grief and love – and their frequent intertwining – as well as the sacrifices that women are compelled to make for love, and the ways in which women might resist, and reclaim themselves – however long after the fact.'

—*The Guardian*

'A moving meta-story … [*The Sitter's*] sophisticated three-part structure supports the tug and pull of these modes: artist and subject, seeing and being seen, telling stories and having your stories told. The second part, which centres on the writer's past, is especially successful. Here, O'Keeffe imbues the writing with dreamlike qualities.'

—*Australian Book Review*

'[A] prismatic story of creativity and observation.'

—*The Saturday Paper*

'Angela O'Keeffe has written a deceptively brief novel that is a muscular and powerful interrogation of the nature of female relationships with each other as well as with as the men in their lives … *The Sitter* is clever and sharp-eyed while also being exquisitely painful, funny and regretful. It truly is a gem of a novel.'

—**Meredith Jaffé**

Angela O'Keeffe grew up with nine siblings on a farm in the Lockyer Valley, Queensland. She completed a Master of Arts in Writing at UTS, and her first novel, *Night Blue*, was shortlisted for the UTS Glenda Adams Award for New Writing and the Prime  Minister's Literary Awards. She was the recipient of the 2023 Varuna Eleanor Dark Fellowship.

THE
SITTER

THE SITTER

A NOVEL

ANGELA O'KEEFFE

ZEROGRAM PRESS

Los Angeles, 2023

Copyright © 2023 by Angela O'keeffe

All rights reserved. No part of this book may be reproduced or transmitted in any form or by any means, electronic or mechanical, including photocopying, recording or storing information in a retrieval system, without prior written permission from the publisher.

First Zerogram Press Edition 2023

ZEROGRAM PRESS
1147 El Medio Ave.
Pacific Palisades, CA 90272
Email: info@zerogrampress.com
Website: www.zerogrampress.com

Distributed by Small Press United / Independent Publishers Group
(800) 888-4741 / www.ipgbook.com

Book Design by Creative Publishing Book Design

ISBN #: 9781953409140

Publisher's Cataloging-in-Publication
(Provided by Cassidy Cataloguing Services, Inc.).
Names: O'Keeffe, Angela, author.
Title: The sitter : a novel / Angela O'Keeffe.
Description: First Zerogram Press edition. | Los Angeles : Zerogram Press,
     2024.
Identifiers: ISBN: 978-1-953409-14-0
Subjects: LCSH: Fiquet, Hortense, 1850-1922--Fiction. | Women authors
     --France--Paris--Fiction. | Adoption--Fiction. | Pandemics
     --Fiction. | Hotels--France--Paris--Fiction.
Classification: LCC: PS3615.K41 S58 2024 | DDC: 813/.6--dc23

Printed in the United States of America

For Caroline and Frida
Loved always

'Shade, too, can be inhabited.'
GASTON BACHELARD, *The Poetics of Space*

PART I

FROM THE WINDOW OF A HOTEL room in Paris: a view of rooftops, the brown river, a cobblestoned street, one corner of a scaffolded, burnt-out church. It is a morning in March 2020 and the air holds a breath of warmth. The sky is a pale, hopeful blue.

Normally on such a morning, a morning that is chilly but nevertheless heralds the first hint of spring, the street would be almost crowded, the mood bordering on flamboyant, as the first hint of spring is more a cause for celebration than spring itself. But this morning, from this window, just three people can be seen in the street. Two women walk side by side, each carrying brown paper bags of groceries, each wearing a blue surgical mask. A small child strides out ahead of them, stopping every now and then to gaze with curiosity at the cobblestones, as if the cobblestones are marvellous, as if the cobblestones possess some secret that will any moment make itself known.

The window through which this scene is being viewed is tall and graceful with a suggestion of something lacking, an almost imperceptible narrowness to the design that suggests, perhaps, that generosity must be tempered with humility. Its glass is clean, flawless except for a crack running from the lower left corner towards the centre, a crack that looks like a lightning bolt – not the zig-zag representation of a lightning bolt, but a real one. It has a real lightning bolt's meandering beauty and unwavering sense of purpose.

The air inside the room is without a season. A temperature gauge, hidden somewhere in the room or in the innards of the building itself, ensures this. The chilly air from outside comes in through the crack in the window, just a little of it, seeking warmth; the neutral air from inside the room wafts out through the crack in the window, just a little of it, seeking adventure. In and out the air goes, in and out.

There are two people in the room. A woman in her sixties stands at the window. She has just taken in the view as I have described it: the two women in the street, their brown paper bags of groceries – from the top of one protrudes something leafy, from another a baguette – the child striding ahead of them full of curiosity and an easy confidence.

The woman at the window has long, greyish-silver hair streaked here and there with black; it looks like the remnants of a fire, soot and half-burnt logs arranged into something smooth and almost pleasing. The sunlight streaming in the window highlights the tiny lines that fan out from the corners of her eyes and around her lips.

The other person in the room is me, Marie-Hortense Fiquet Cezanne. You may recognise my last name. Yes, *that* Cezanne. The French painter Paul Cezanne (1839–1906) was my husband. Arguably most famous for painting apples, he painted my portrait far more times than he ever painted apples. Twenty-nine times to be exact. It is March 2020 and I am here, in this hotel with the woman with the silver-black hair and the lined lips, in the city where I worked as a bookbinder and an artist's model over a hundred years ago, where I met my husband and gave birth to our son, and where I spent backbreaking hours sitting for my husband as he painted my portrait, while the sky slid by through the window, blinking day, blinking night. The birds in that sky were always happy. As I sat, I had thoughts – such as this observation about birds – that never made it into any one of those portraits.

My husband used to say that if he couldn't find in himself a *feeling* for a part of the subject he was painting, then he was compelled to leave that section of the painting blank. In the portraits of me there are many blanks.

I am here in Paris; I keep reiterating this. Do I fear that any moment the fact might be taken from me? The city where I lived from the age of eight, on and off, until my death in 1922. My grave is here, in Père Lachaise Cemetery, where in summer the trees are weighted with brightness and children play hide and seek among the headstones.

But I am not interested in graves; I am not interested in death. At least, not as much as I am interested in the woman standing beside me at the window, who draws from me a strange desire that glitters and tumbles like a ball in a game, just out of reach.

The woman is a writer. She is writing a novel about me. The novel is in its early stage, 'the scrappy notes and bits of magic stage', she calls it. She is compiling the scrappy notes and bits of magic on her laptop, and almost every day of the nearly three weeks that we have been here in France she has added to them.

The first two weeks were spent eight hours' drive south, in Aix-en-Provence, the town where my husband grew up and where he lived and painted for most of his life. The writer rented an Airbnb with a view of Mont Sainte-Victoire, the stark, brooding mountain that sits just beyond the town, a mountain that my husband painted thirty-six times in oil and forty-five times in watercolour.

You will notice that I like to keep count. I'm not sure why, but there has always been a kind of contest in my mind. A contest between me and the mountain, a contest between me and the apples, a contest between me and Cezanne himself – for he painted his own portrait even more times than he painted mine. I never enjoyed having my portrait painted; I found the sitting tiring, tedious and mostly thankless work. Added to that, my husband was a slow painter; his brush would hover in the air for twenty maddening minutes or more as he looked from me to the canvas, from the canvas to me, attempting to find, or *feel*, his way to the next brushstroke, while outside the window the birds flew or sang or slept.

In the portraits I look unhappy, many people have said this, and I admit I am no Mona Lisa; in not one is there even the hint of a smile on my lips. In some I scarcely have lips at all. But don't be deceived by this simple conclusion, even if it is true. There is a thrill to unhappiness that most people do not understand.

During the weeks we spent in Aix, the manuscript grew and diminished on the writer's laptop. Some days she pushed and frowned her way through paragraphs that were deleted almost as quickly as they appeared; on others the words rushed through her like light, and her fingers on the keyboard were scarcely able to keep up. As she wrote I stood by her side, gazing down at her silvery-black hair, feeling parts of myself break free and flow into some invisible sea that was beyond us both.

One morning she looked up from her computer and murmured, 'It's going to be alright, Hortense. It's going to be a book.' Through the window the mountain glowed dimly in the cold light. I was sitting across from her at the tiny kitchen table, for when I grew weary of standing by her side, I would sit to face her, watching the lines on her face as she wrote my story – lines configured around her features, sunken between her bones. Lines that I thought might tell their own story, one day.

'I should think so,' I said.

'What do you mean, *I should think so*?' She looked amused, raising one thin brow.

'I mean, you're spending a lot of time and money to be here, in Aix – a place I detest,' I added.

'I know it's not easy for you here,' she said, and reached across the table to take my hand – or would have, if I had a hand to take, for I am a bodiless presence. I sit without sitting; I speak without speaking. Yet I have a voice; you, for one, can hear it, and so can the writer, at least some of the time.

She looked back to the screen then, her attention once again on the manuscript, on the words assembling and disassembling like rows of surf.

In Aix she spent the mornings writing and the afternoons walking on the trails near Mont Sainte-Victoire, stopping for long moments to stare at a tree, at a tuft of grass, at the mountain itself. On these walks a space opened between us. She strode out ahead; I lagged behind. I am more aware of this space now, days later, as I stand at the window beside her here in Paris and watch the two masked women and the child walk below us in the street. Nevertheless, it struck me at the time. It was more than a physical space; it was a space of feeling, a space that, I think now, pointed to some new understanding between us.

I remember her turning to me one day as she walked on a trail near the very foot of the mountain. There was a large pine tree behind her, and she stood in its dappled shade. 'Hortense, come on!' she coaxed, and I tried with all my might to make my way to her. I stumbled without stumbling; my muscles ached without aching; my breathless breath grew ragged. But all to no avail. The distance, and the shade cast by the tree, conspired to make her face a blur to me. I could not discern its individual lines. It was a face with no history that I could detect.

She would leave the house for these walks wearing a hat that had once belonged to her husband, who was dead. 'Now where is Malcolm's hat?' she'd murmur as she readied herself to go out, searching first in the kitchen, where her laptop lay in repose after its morning exertions, then in the other rooms: the bedroom, the lounge room, the bathroom. The hat could have been in any of these rooms, as when she wasn't sitting at her computer writing or lying on the couch reading or standing at the sink eating – she seldom sat to eat, she was too full of fidgety words – she was in the habit of drifting through the rooms with a demeanour that reminded me of my son when he'd walked in his sleep as a child, and in that state she would put things down in any old place. She is not forgetful – at least, not in the ordinary sense. She can, for instance, remember with remarkable precision the dates and events that punctuate my life. She has no affliction, as far as I can tell, except for a one-pointed attention to her own inner world to the exclusion of all else; once, she came across her hairbrush in the fridge.

The hat is a wide-brimmed, battered specimen made of felt, far too big for her – she could comfortably wear a beanie underneath. In addition, she dressed for these walks in pink runners, thick woollen socks, track pants, a woollen skivvy, a knitted jumper, a puffer jacket, gloves and a scarf. The first time I saw her dressed like this I laughed. 'We're in the south. The winters are mild. It rarely ever snows in Aix.'

She shrugged as she opened the front door. 'It was summer in Sydney when we left.'

I met her at the beginning of that summer, in the beachside suburb of Bondi, around the time she began writing the novel about me. I don't know exactly how I made my way to that room in her house near the roaring Pacific. There was an event that preceded my arrival, but for all that I was simply there one morning, standing in the doorway watching as she sat at her desk, her back to me, the sun shining through the window onto her head. A harsh sun. Sydney is a crushed and glittering prism of light.

As I stepped into the room I was startled by the call of a bird from outside, a raucous sound, like an old and angry man clearing his throat.

'Don't mind the cockatoos,' she said, as I came towards her. She turned in her chair and I gazed into her lined face with its shining eyes, eyes that made me nervous from the start, for they seemed to know everything about me and at the same time nothing at all.

'My name is Hortense,' I said, a thrill running through me; I had spoken in English, a language I had not known in life.

It was then that I became aware of the sea. Though not visible through the window, I could smell its seaweed smell, I could hear its roar of outrage – for the sea is a constant agitator for change, for resetting, for rewriting old rules. *If you want a quiet life, don't live by the sea*, I thought, and I wondered why I had thought this, as I had hardly ever lived by the sea. Then I wondered if the idea had come to me from her. For already there was a kind of porousness between us, when I looked at her, and she looked at me.

Those days in Sydney were structured the opposite to how our days in Aix would be. She rose early and walked by the sea, and I went with her, the air warm and soft. We followed the path to the south of Bondi Beach, which weaves above the cliffs, the waves smashing on the sandstone rocks below. There were other walkers as well as joggers on the path, most wearing headphones, shutting out the sea in favour of some other sound.

The sandstone rocks were beautiful. Now and then the writer stopped to watch them, the waves washing over making them darker, the sun on their bare backs making them lighter – darker, lighter, darker, lighter. Once, she stopped so suddenly that a jogger had to swerve abruptly to avoid running into her. 'Grow a brain,' he muttered, before running on. I couldn't help but think that my husband would've loved these rocks, that *he* would've stopped and stared at them just as she did.

You have probably noticed that I seldom refer to my husband by his name. He is simply 'my husband'. This makes him more mine than if I were to call him by his name. Paul Cezanne belongs to everyone. But *my husband* belongs to me.

It would be midmorning by the time she returned to the house, showered, ate breakfast, and went into her cool, white-walled study to sit down to write. Sometimes, before opening her laptop, she chose a book from a twisted pile on the floor near her desk and pored over passages about my husband's art and life, underlining sentences and writing comments in the margins.

Watching over her shoulder, I noted that there was little about me in these books, and that if I was mentioned at all it was rarely in a complimentary way. In one passage, for example, my husband's friend Paul Alexis referred to me as 'La Boule' (the ball), because of my full and, to him, unattractive figure. Others said that I had never understood or appreciated Cezanne's art, that I was a troublemaker, a money-grubber and a drunk. There was a story that after my mother-in-law died I made a bonfire of her possessions; another that I refused to come to my husband's deathbed because of 'a pressing engagement' with my dressmaker. I am tempted to deny it all, to try to clear my name, but the truth is I recognise the woman portrayed in these flimsy accounts, just as one recognises one's own face in a stream: the shifting water and sunlight playing with the reflection, both revealing and disguising it.

Perhaps I do not want to clear my name. Perhaps I want much more than that.

It was during those days in Sydney that I developed a habit of standing at the writer's shoulder while she worked. I grew accustomed to the tap of her fingers on the keyboard, to the sound of the air going in and out of her lungs, and the slight rise and fall of her chest; it all seemed a way into the rhythm of her feelings, and each day I felt myself edging closer to her. Sometimes my gaze drifted to the window, to the paperbarks and banksias in her garden, in which there were often cockatoos, their yellow crests like fragments of sun. I was no longer startled by their screeches.

A sense of reassurance began to creep over me in the days before we caught the plane, together, to France. The warm summer air, the flow of her days, her fingers on the keyboard – all had a lulling effect. As the sentences took shape, she posed questions to me without speaking, and I answered without speaking back. Yet, in a strange contradiction, she sometimes ignored my answers, just as she ignored the cockatoos' screeches. From the start there was an evasiveness, a kind of undertow, that made me wonder if the story would turn out right.

That summer, every state in Australia was ravaged by bushfires. I soon discovered that the clear bright sky of my first days in Bondi had simply been a reprieve, that the smoke from the fires near the city had in fact been blowing the other way. When the wind changed direction and the smoke returned, it created a grey pall over the city the thickness of which I had not witnessed, even during long-ago winters in Paris when the smoke from fireplaces cast a thick cloud. It hung like cobwebs in the paperbarks in the writer's garden; it made a charcoal drawing of our morning walks, a drawing in which the sky and the sea were fused. Walkers and joggers moved with a strange viscosity, snippets of their conversations like flotsam. There were complaints of difficulty breathing, of itchy eyes, of washing hung on the line only to be stained by soot, of burnt leaves raining into gardens.

It feels like the world is ending.

And we can't do anything. We're *watching*.

We're not just watching; we're *in* it.

Did you see those people who escaped in boats and watched as their town burnt?

The sky was beautiful.

And horrifying; it was the middle of the *day*.

It was night.

Whatever, it was spectacular.

Billions of animals killed, *billions.* Thirty-three people – that's bad, but for god's sake, those *animals.*

And the plants: *millions of hectares.*

I can't get my head around it.

No-one can.

Welcome to 2020.

Each night on the news there were images of fires burning across forests, burning through towns, burning to the edge of the sea. There were reports that some of the fires had been deliberately lit. 'I suppose they do it for the power,' murmured the writer to someone over the phone, and I thought of the fire I had lit to burn my mother-in-law's possessions. The flames had been tiny at first, half smothered by the garments I'd dragged into the courtyard, the dresses and nightgowns that smelt of camphor, before I threw on some old newspapers and the fire leapt to life. I wasn't sure that I had done it for the power. But if I had, it was a power that lived not in me but in the flames themselves.

Since childhood, the writer had suffered from asthma, and now on her walks she wore a P2 mask and carried a puffer. When her breathing became like that of a horse pulling a cart up a hill – that is, when it unexpectedly quietened towards some inner labour – she would remove the mask and hold the puffer to her mouth and draw a decisive breath. Her daughter, Rebecca, implored her to stay in the house on the days of heavy smoke, but the writer insisted, 'I can't be cooped up.'

In February she packed her bags. By then the fires were over, though they were still being discussed every night on the television: how to rebuild towns, livelihoods and the ecology; what action should be taken on climate change; and what could be done about the psychological and economic effects on a population that has been on high alert all summer, people not knowing when or if their homes would need to be evacuated, their businesses and workplaces closed.

'I'll be glad to get to France,' she said, folding a woollen scarf and placing it in the open suitcase on her bed, 'and leave this catastrophe behind me.'

And now the writer and I are standing at the window of this hotel room in Paris, the three figures walking below us in the street. There begins a faint, mechanical wail, weak but quickly gaining momentum and a sense of urgency – a wail that I cannot help but associate with the one that issued from my own lips, long ago, when I was told that my husband was dead.

I'd stepped off a train in Aix and was given the news – but I will come back to this; I will tell you about his death. Not that death is my main interest here – I have already stated this – but death is a means of turning towards life; death is a compass. As I stand at the window with the writer, and down in the street the child looks lovingly at the cobblestones upon which the weak morning light casts a sheen, and the wail becomes ever louder, I must, briefly, say something about the last hundred years.

For one hundred years I was dead – or asleep. Call it what you wish. I lay in the arms of the dear, dark earth in Père Lachaise Cemetery, where I dreamt of my own fingers sewing together the pages of a book; where I dreamt of dresses and brushstrokes; where I dreamt of turning towards a window and murmuring, 'Dear little birds,' and my husband's voice upon me like a landslide – 'Ne bouge pas! Ne parle pas!' *Don't move! Don't speak!*

They were not outlandish dreams, by any means, for I am a realist at heart.

Until one day I awoke. And found myself standing in a large white room. On its walls were paintings. A dozen or so people moved about the room in ones, twos, groups. I glanced at the painting nearest to me. It took me a moment to recognise it as one of the twenty-nine portraits. *Madame Cezanne in a Red Armchair.* Painted in 1877, it is one of the few portraits in which my lips are full. In it I am given, almost, the capacity to speak.

The people in the room drifted languidly, gazing at this painting, and this. What struck me about them initially was the design of their clothing: skimpy, tight garments in lurid colours, shoes that fitted snugly without buckles or laces – all in stark contrast to the designs of my era. It was my first hint as to the length of time I had slept.

And now a man and a woman approached to stand before *Madame Cezanne in a Red Armchair*. As the woman studied the portrait, she came very close beside me, and I felt her breath disrupt the still air.

'She's a beauty,' she said in English. Though impressed that I understood, I was hardly surprised; it was like the sensation of dreaming of rain and then waking to find that it really is raining.

'Are you kidding me?' the man with her said.

'You don't know what beauty is,' she said, without taking her gaze from the portrait.

'Clearly.'

'I could take that as an insult.'

'There's no winning with you.'

'Rilke loved her. When this painting was exhibited, over a century ago, he went back time and again to look at her.'

'Good for him.'

She took a breath and turned to him, her gaze soft as a petal. 'I'm leaving you.'

'You're ... what?'

'I saw the card on your desk.' Her gaze was no longer soft, but open, like a wound. 'I went to your study to water the plant, the one you never water, and I saw it.'

He blinked. 'Oh.' He looked at the floor, then back at her. 'We have to talk.'

'We're talking.'

'Not here.' He went to take her arm, but she twisted out of reach, and then together they walked to the doorway at the far end of the room.

My husband and I had frequent arguments, our voices cutting through the darkness of our bedroom. Sometimes one of us packed a bag and stepped out into the night. For my part, I would take our son and stay with my dressmaker. The boy would fall asleep in my lap while I sat at her table as she worked, calmed by the croak of her scissors and her voice muffled by the pins she held between her lips.

I don't know where my husband went when he left. But mostly when we fought, we each stayed exactly where we were, surly and steadfast. We'd spend weeks hardly speaking, and our son would act as go-between: 'Papa, Mama says dinner is ready,' and so on. Through it all my husband painted, and I kept house. Because of financial restraints we didn't always have paid help; I did the cooking, the cleaning and the washing of his workspace, his clothes, his paintbrushes; I wrote letters to his dealer to organise the sale of paintings; I was his assistant, his housekeeper, his secretary, his lover, his model and – though in the books about him few writers seem willing to consider this, perhaps because he himself never named me as such – his muse. We were not equals. He had the power to throw me out on my ear, the power to never give me another franc; at a certain point he changed his will and disinherited me, though by the end of his life he'd made sure that I would receive something.

And yet.

There were times when all I had to do was look at him and he would reel under my gaze. He'd go to his paints, his hands shaking, and take up the brush, saying in a compliant rather than commanding tone – as if he were obeying me – 'Hortense, sit.'

It was the shadow side of power. Some possess it as easily as the air they breathe, while others go their whole lives not knowing such a thing exists.

Back at the gallery, after the couple had walked away, night fell, and the room emptied and the lights dimmed. I was left alone to study the woman in the portrait, the woman who was me and yet not me. I remembered how it felt to sit for that portrait, the throbbing stiffness that accumulated in my neck, my shoulders, my lower back; I remembered the longing for each day to end, for the moment when I could stand and stretch my body, my spine curving, twisting, my arms reaching upward, my fingers raking the thin air. Yet when that moment came, as my husband turned from the canvas and murmured that he was finished for the day – in that moment, I, about to stand, would hesitate, the way an animal released from a cage hesitates before crossing the threshold, and I would think of the chores that awaited me, the cooking, the cleaning, and making sure our son was bathed; I would think of the morose atmosphere between my husband and me and the space between us in our bed – and I would wish that I did not have to stand at all, but rather that I could slip from the chair, oblivious, into some other world.

All through that night I watched the woman Rilke had returned to look at, again and again. All was quiet and still, the silence broken only by a guard who padded by intermittently, deep in his own thoughts.

Then I heard the short clear call of a bird, and morning light came in. Before me the woman's lips quivered – and I felt myself slipping, just as I had once longed to, and seconds or perhaps years later there I stood in the doorway of the writer's study.

In Aix, she heard – first from the owner of the Airbnb, who lived next door; then from her daughter, who frequently emailed and phoned from Sydney; and then from various news sites she watched on her laptop, which she began to check with increasing frequency – that an illness was spreading, that the death toll was rising, that borders were shutting.

'What is this illness?' I asked her one morning at dawn. She sat at her laptop in her pyjamas, a woollen shawl around her shoulders. A lamp shone in the corner. Through the window, in the greyness, I could just make out the ungainly shape of the mountain my husband loved so much. No. Not love. It wasn't love that he felt for the things that he was compelled to paint. It was something beyond love, something that made an excuse of love – although I have no proof of this. I have no proof of any of it.

The writer looked up from the screen on which she'd been writing sentences about my husband and me. She'd been writing specifically about how we did not marry until our son was a teenager; how my husband had kept the existence of our child from his father, who was a banker in Aix and who may have cut off my husband's allowance, on which we survived, had he known of the disgrace. The problem wasn't simply that we'd had a child out of wedlock, but that I was not a suitable choice. My father was a poor farmer and a bookbinder. I was not from a class fit for a banker's son.

'It's a virus, a kind of flu,' she said.

A flu? My attention quickened. 'I lived through a very bad flu.'

'It kills older people, mostly,' she said.

'The flu I remember killed the young.'

My dressmaker lost a granddaughter, a girl of eighteen, to the Spanish flu. I'd taken soup to the girl while she was sick, but it went untouched, for by then she had the telltale dark-red spot on each cheek. Death was close. Her eyes were large and glowed with a weariness so intense it filled the room in which she lay, touching its walls, its floor, its ceiling. I felt its force as I stood beside her bed holding the bowl of useless soup, and I knew it would be easy to mistake this great, glowing weariness for courage. But I did not mistake it.

'It was a cruel illness,' I said now, but she wasn't listening. She'd closed the manuscript and opened an email from her daughter.

Although I died in 1922, I am cognisant when it comes to computers – at least, I am as cognisant as the writer herself. This is reasonable; I am a combination of the *me* I once was when I lived, and the *me* that the writer cannot help but give bits of herself to. In this way I am the *me* that I never was before, the *me* of some new potential.

She drew the woollen shawl around her shoulders; the shawl had been knitted by her mother decades before and she'd kept it all these years. One day she told me that it is the item of clothing she cherishes above all others. Even so, she treats it shabbily. It is like a child's favourite blanket: lived in, breathed on, cried upon. It is often left lying on the floor. With the shawl around her shoulders, she read the email from her daughter.

> Mum, you have to come home. They are talking about closing the border. Change your flight. I heard from Francis's cousin, who's just managed to return from London, that flights were disappearing on the screen before him, and prices climbing. You have to change your ticket.

The next morning, she packed the car early and we left Aix, passing through the streets of yellow buildings in the town centre, streets that I'd walked through in the days before my wedding with a feeling of meek rage. I wasn't good enough; I was *better* than good enough: these opposing thoughts pounded into my every step. At the wedding ceremony, which took place in the town hall in Aix, my mother-in-law smiled and took my hand, but her eyes were without warmth. Her husband turned away from me. He died a few months after the wedding, and I was filled with a sense of vindication, which I carried with me through the streets of Paris to my dressmaker's, intent on spending as many of the francs that he had left my husband as I could on dresses of fine silk. The sense of vindication ran down my arm and into my fingers whenever I wrote a letter and signed it *Madame Cezanne*.

Do you see what I mean by there being a thrill to unhappiness?

We arrived in Paris towards the end of that day – three days ago now – and checked into this hotel, which overlooks the burnt-out church of Notre-Dame. Scaffolded in steel and missing its spire, it is a sorry sight.

'What happened to the church?' I asked after she went to the window and pulled back the curtains, and there we stood together for the first time, looking out.

I was reminded of the many times my husband and I had arrived in a new place, for we'd moved around a lot, within Paris and across the country. When we arrived somewhere new he would go to the window, just as the writer had, and pull back the curtains to let in the light. But rather than looking out at the view, he would turn inwards towards the room itself, surveying its contents with his pointed gaze, and his mood would shift accordingly. If the light fell against the objects in the room in a promising way, he would set to work, sorting brushes and pots of paint; sometimes he would pause to look at me, to take in my features as if they held some vital information (he was always snatching at information). If the fall of the light did not please him, he would slump in a chair and bemoan his bad luck; he would stare through me as if I were made of glass, and it would take all my skill to convince him to let food or drink pass his lips. I would prepare the meal from whatever I had managed to buy along the way – bread, cheese, wine – laying the table as prettily as I could: if possible, finding a vase to fill with fresh flowers. I would wear my best dress, leaving my hair loose, the way he liked it when we made love. I would keep our son as quiet as I could, for my husband could not endure what he termed 'unnecessary noise'.

The writer gestured to the church. 'There was a fire,' she said.

'The spire is gone,' I said.

'It fell in.'

'Do the bells still ring?'

'No, they are being fixed.'

'I remember going into Notre-Dame long ago,' I said, my voice taking on a dreamy quality, almost as if it were not my own – yet it was more my own than it ever was. 'The bells were ringing for mass. I lit a candle and put it with the other candles, burning and flickering in rows, burning for the sick, for the dying, for the dead.'

The writer said nothing, and we both continued to look outside.

There were quite a few people in the street that first day in Paris. People still moved with an air of unrestraint; shops and cafés were open. Families drifted along the streets, little breaths of colour and life. The only thing that hinted at what was to come was that here and there was an individual wearing a face mask, and I was reminded of the masks worn during the Spanish flu; I'd worn them myself, made by my dressmaker from layers of leftover calico.

It was almost dusk. The sun withdrew quickly from the cobblestones and along the sides of the buildings.

'I didn't stay for mass,' I went on, though she wasn't listening. She was watching a family – a man, a woman and two little girls – taking a selfie in front of Notre-Dame. The man held his phone at arm's length and moved it this way, that way, trying to fit them all into the frame. The woman said something, and the little girls began to laugh. The man laughed too.

'After I lit the candle, I walked home along the river and watched the rats,' I said. 'Did you know that if you look fondly at a rat, it stops its constant shiver?'

The words that come from me when I am with the writer sometimes surprise me, yet as I say them I know that they are true. I *did* watch the rats. It is as if the skin is peeled from me when I am with her, and I find some truer skin beneath.

Still, she said nothing. The photo had been taken now and the family was moving away, the little girls running off ahead, the man and woman following with heads bowed in conversation. I studied the writer's profile as she watched them, observing that her nose is long and aquiline. My mother would have admired this nose. She used to say that such a nose knew the secrets of refinement, though what those secrets were she never let on. She worked in a big house in the town where I was born; she could polish silver until it offered a curved, discordant mirror to the world; she could heat an iron on a stove to just the right temperature so that it flattened but did not burn the silk of a dress. She could serve those whom she considered her betters, and mutter beneath her breath when those betters turned their backs. She could hold her head high when she walked in the street, as if *her* clothes were made of silk instead of cotton.

In some way all this rubbed off on me.

A shudder went through the writer as she watched the family move off. She sneezed, and reached into the pocket of her track pants for a tissue. And sneezed again, her head jerking forward so that her hair came across her face. She tucked it behind each ear, blew her nose then went into the bathroom, and I was left alone at the window. The sun had receded completely, leaving a pall of grey light that lasted some minutes, a suspension between day and night. Then in fits and starts the lights of Paris came on.

I should explain why I call her 'the writer'. It is not because I need to remind myself that she is writing a book. From the start of my time with her the book has dogged my every step.

No. It is because I do not know her name. I have heard it, of course; others call her by her name; she calls herself by her name, when answering the phone or checking into a hotel, for instance. But when I hear her name it enters me in camouflage. It's like white ink on a white page; it's like tears cried into the sea. She is less a person to me than she is a function: she writes.

Yet I am curious about her. More, it must be said, than I am curious about the book. I study her features, her expressions, her habits, I observe her as she writes, as she imagines my life, a life that at times I can scarcely imagine myself; there it is, behind me, glimmering in parts, grotesque in others, a landscape I am no longer a part of, but that I diligently bring to her, over and over, scraping up handfuls of dust and laying them at her feet. Though she is pleased by these offerings, they are never enough; she sighs and looks despondent, like a child who longs for a toy then when she gets it wants something else.

On that first afternoon in the hotel, she returned from the bathroom with her hair up in a ponytail, which I thought made her look younger, almost childlike, except that it accentuated the sagging skin beneath her chin. Coming to the window she murmured, 'Ah, the lights', and put her hands on her hips, which are narrow, like a boy's – the kind of hips my mother, ever attuned to the snares of giving birth, would have labelled 'troublesome'.

It was then that I first noticed the crack in the window, just beyond where she stood. It ran from the edge of the window towards its centre, fine as a human hair, fine as the distance between us – for I am part of her, and she is part of me.

Her phone vibrated on the bedside table. In one seamless movement she crossed the room, picked it up and lay flat out on her back on the white bedspread, her pink runners still on her feet.

'Darling.'

'Mum.'

She held the phone above her like a mirror as she looked into the face of her daughter, Rebecca.

'Did you get a flight?'

'I did.'

'When are you coming?'

'In a week.'

'A *week*.'

'It's the best I could do.'

'Are you lying down? Your face looks smooth.'

'A good look for the old.'

'You're not old.'

'I almost am.'

'I'll meet you.'

'Thanks, darling, but there's no need.'

'I want to.'

'Actually, I don't think it's allowed. I read they're bringing in home quarantine.'

'Oh, yeah, of course. You'll have to get an Uber.'

'What if I give it to the Uber driver?'

'What if they give it to you?'

'It looks dreadful in Italy – they say it will soon be like that here in France. Is that a new blouse?'

'It's the silk one with the stars – I've had it since before Dad died.'

'Oh yes, I know it. Have you noticed that his death is a kind of marker for us? Everything is either *before* or *after*.'

'It's true.'

'If he were alive, we could go into quarantine together. We'd sit in the garden, reading, like we used to. Me in my shawl. Him in his old hat. I brought the shawl and the hat away with me. I must be getting sentimental.' She paused. 'I've had that shawl since I was sixteen, you know. Mum knitted it for me.'

'Yes, I know. I always thought it was a weird thing to knit for a teenager.'

'Oh, it wasn't weird. Shawls were all the rage then. Joni Mitchell wore shawls.'

'When did Dad get the hat?'

'He bought it years ago, at that milliner's in the city. It wasn't cheap. He wanted a good one.'

'I have no memory of him in any other hat.'

'It's a bit battered, but it's lasted.'

They stared past one another for a moment, and then the daughter said, 'Remember what we talked about the night before you flew to France?'

The writer gave a start so tiny that it registered only at the corners of her eyes before it was gone. 'Well, we talked about a lot of things that night. We talked about possums, I recall.'

'I mean the thing you told me, about you and Dad. You'd never told me that before.'

'No, I hadn't.'

Again, they stared past one another, and then the daughter said, 'Can you tell me about it?'

The writer spoke in a quiet voice. 'Now?'

Rebecca looked at her closely. 'When you come home – if you'd rather.'

'Alright. Bec, you should see the lights from my window.'

'I hope you're not planning on going out.'

The writer laughed. 'I'm in *Paris.*'

'Mum, this thing is so contagious.'

'I know. But I have to … live.'

'My point exactly.'

'I'll be sensible.'

'Being sensible is staying put.'

'Darling, I'm really tired. Do you mind if I go now?'

'Of course not. You know I'm only bossy because I love you.'

'I love you too.'

She let the phone fall on the bedcover and sighed, the air expending with a faint wheeze, and then she turned, and I felt her attention on me. A feeling of warmth flowed through me. *I live by her attention*, I thought. *I have come to depend on it.*

'Who did you light the candle for in Notre-Dame?'
she asked.

So, she had been listening.

The room was golden, and a shadow lay across the
bed, dissecting her thin body. *The shadow of the spire*, I
thought, but then I remembered that Notre-Dame no
longer had a spire, that the spire had fallen in.

I tried to remember who I'd lit the candle for. But it
was as if the person's face was being erased in my mind
by the very effort I was making to remember it, in the
same way that our dreams hide from us upon our waking
if we study them too hard.

'I don't know,' I said.

With a century of sleep behind me I have no need of
it; I lie awake in the silken night. That first night in the
hotel the writer stayed awake too. She hadn't closed the
curtains and the city's lights shone in. She lay in their
glow, staring at the ceiling as if it contained some riddle
that she needed to turn over in her mind, and I found
myself watching her. My thoughts, which usually roam
far and wide as she sleeps, were still, breathless. At last,
as dawn broke, she fell asleep, curled like a kitten, one
hand beneath her chin, and my mind was released to its
pacing back and forth.

I thought of my days as a bookbinder, working along-
side my father in a small, dilapidated room at the back

of a music shop in Paris. I used to walk through the shop to get to work, and the instruments – violins, guitars and cellos – watched me with their polished cunning, making me wonder if inanimate objects could know more about my life, about my secrets, about my future, than I did myself.

It was in a park near the bookbinder's that I met my husband. I sat on a bench in the sun, while around me trees were in blossom. My fingers were sore from a morning spent sewing pages, and I held them up to the light; I held them up to the perfumed flowers.

He came and sat beside me. I didn't see him approach; he was suddenly there, close. His brown eyes were soft, and he smelt of paint. He asked me to lay my hands in my lap; I thought it an odd request, but I did as he asked. I was used to a teasing amusement in the voices of men, particularly those who wanted what my mother called 'one thing', but his voice had none of that. His voice had a deep seriousness that seemed to come as much out of need as out of desire; in him, need and desire were stitched together, bound like the pages of a book.

'Can I paint you?' he almost whispered.

He did not ask my name, and I did not ask his.

And I thought of my mother standing at the mirror doing her hair into a twist at the nape of her neck. Me, a child, looking up: 'Mama, why do you hide your hair from yourself?' Her pause, looking down, her elbows like wings: 'You're a funny little thing, Hortense.'

And I thought of what Rebecca had said on the phone to the writer earlier that night – *the thing you told me, about you and Dad* – and how the writer had given a tiny start. As she slept on, the back of one hand against her chin in what I thought was an uncharacteristically graceful gesture, I went over the conversation that had taken place at Rebecca's house on our last night in Sydney.

Though the night was clear in my memory, I could not recall the part of the conversation that Rebecca had referred to. *The thing you told me, about you and Dad.* This did not strike me as particularly odd. I have not been in the habit of noticing *everything* she says or does. From the beginning, there have been blanks.

But what we do not notice about an experience leaves a shadow in our mind, it seems to me – the shadow of what we might have noticed had we paid attention. And it was for such a shadow that I now searched.

She'd walked to Rebecca's house, just blocks from her own, the air clear and warm and indulgent; it seemed a reassurance that the fires were over, that the catastrophe of the summer was past.

After the meal of spaghetti bolognaise and salad, a favourite of her grandson, Lucas, the writer read the boy a bedtime story. The writer's voice had a sing-song quality; the air in the room was still and soft. Lucas hugged a toy to his cheek. Eventually his eyes grew heavy, and he fell asleep.

For a time she sat gazing at him, a tiny smile on her lips, and I remembered watching my sleeping son in this same way, as if all of my hopes were compressed beneath his shut lids.

She slipped out of the room and came onto the balcony to join Rebecca. With wineglasses in hand they sat side by side on the limestone deck.

'It's hard to believe I'll be somewhere cold in a couple of days,' she said, looking down at her bare feet.

A movement in a nearby tree: a pair of bright eyes. Then more movement, rustling of branches; the eyes were gone.

'A possum!' Rebecca spoke with quiet excitement.

'They're a nuisance,' the writer said and sipped her wine.

'Mum, that's … heartless.'

'Oh, for god's sake. I don't *hate* them.' She bent and put her glass at her feet. 'It's just that your father and I had such trouble with them in our roof.'

'Really?'

'It must have been when you were in Boston. We had to get the possum piper to come and get them out.'

'The possum piper.' Rebecca smiled. 'Did they play music and make the possums march away after them?'

'Not quite. They patched up the holes that led into the roof, holes that the possums had apparently been getting in and out of. They'd been sleeping in the roof by day and going out to feed at night. The possum piper patched up all the holes but one, which they fitted with a little metal door. The door only worked one way.' A stillness came over the writer's face as she spoke; her eyes were pinched, her lips bright. 'They put the one-way door on the last remaining hole, so that the possums could get out to feed, but when they returned, they couldn't get back in.'

She stared into the tree where the possum had been. All was still. The sea roared far off in the quietness.

After a moment, she went on. 'The possum piper told us that sometimes, if there are babies in the possum family, the parents leave the babies in the roof while they go out to feed. In which case, when the door is blocked, the babies are stuck inside.'

'Oh, that's horrible,' Rebecca said.

'In the days and nights that followed we were to listen out for babies. If we heard scratching sounds, we were to contact the possum piper so that they could come back and rescue them.'

'Did you hear anything?' Rebecca's voice was almost a whisper.

'No. But it worried me for a while.'

She walked home from Rebecca's through the half-lit streets with her arms folded. The air now had an intimation of the cooler hours ahead. Once inside, she busied herself with the last preparations for catching the plane to France the next morning: she dumped some limp vegetables into the bin and wiped out the fridge; she wheeled the bins out to the kerb (Rebecca was to wheel them in after the collection later in the week). She added to her suitcase the books she was taking. She packed her headphones, phone charger, toiletries, passport, and lay a tracksuit and underwear over the chair near the bed to wear the next morning. She weighed her suitcase by hoisting it, awkwardly, onto the bathroom scales. Finally, sitting on the edge of the bed in her nightie, she leant forward and opened the white cupboard beside the bed. I had never seen her open that cupboard before. The drawer above it, yes – the drawer that contained a tiny bottle of lavender oil that she dabbed on her arms and face to ward off mosquitoes, and a tangle of cords from which she sometimes extricated headphones to listen to music before sleep, and a jar of Vicks in case she woke, coughing, in the night – but not the cupboard.

She reached in and felt around, and now her hand came out holding a small box. Its wood was dark and had an oily smoothness. She lifted the lid, silver hinges glimmered, and I drew closer; I was as curious about what was in that box as I had been about anything in her life. But she closed the lid.

'It's nothing to do with you,' she said, not unkindly, but with a weary patience, and a stillness came into her face – the same stillness, I thought, that had come into it earlier when she'd spoken about the possums. She returned the box to its place in the cupboard and turned out the light.

In Paris that first morning she slept late, and when she woke the sun was warm on the bed. She went to the bathroom, came back naked and sat at the edge of the mattress, her computer on her lap, and proceeded to write, her breasts pale pendulums; one has a tiny scar along its edge, on the tender skin below the underarm. I've never mentioned the scar but I've wanted to; it is proof of the life she has lived beyond me, a life I find myself longing to know about, just as I long to know what is in the little box she took from her bedside cupboard. Her life with her husband, her life with her daughter, her life with her grandchild, her life with her other books: all these I have wondered about. But when she speaks of this life, I don't always listen. I'm not sure why. It's not that I feel bored or distracted, but rather that I feel nothing at all.

Am I like my husband? If I cannot *feel* a part of the subject I am observing, am I compelled to leave that part blank?

As she worked, I stood, as usual, at her side. The sky through the window was blue and bright. I felt a sense of optimism as I watched the words assemble in neat rows; any misgivings I'd had about the book were like petals, almost weightless and easily brushed aside.

She wrote about the day I'd found a letter in a drawer in my husband's studio. I remembered the incident well. I'd been searching for a note from his dealer, Vollard, which had listed some prices for recent works. I was trying to ascertain how much money would be coming in. It was said that I was a spendthrift, and perhaps I was. I couldn't resist beautiful dresses; I always chose the better bottle of wine – if these are the marks of a spendthrift then that is what I was.

Spendthrift. I like the feel of the word, the thud of it on my tongue, a word I could not have known, back then – a word from the writer's own tongue. It has landed on mine now, a kind of kiss.

This is how she worked on the book. This is how I gave her what she didn't know she wanted: she reached out, and I carried her reaching-outness inside me; I carried it, growing fat.

Below are the words we wrote together on that first, blue-sky morning in this room.

> The drawer was a mess of letters. Hortense could not recall it being so untidy. She supposed that her husband had been through it. Perhaps he'd been looking for the same letter that she was; perhaps he'd wanted to sit and brood, as he sometimes did, over the paltry number of his works that Vollard had managed to sell.
>
> The corner of a page in a strange hand, not Vollard's, not her husband's, not her own. A flowery, childish hand.
>
> *My darling Paul*, it said
> *I lie awake thinking of you.*
>
> That was all. It was not signed, which made it all the clearer, to Hortense. He would know who it was from.
> *I lie awake thinking of you.*

That night she lay awake thinking of who might have written the letter. She watched his sleeping face in the bed beside her, his beak-like nose, his broad forehead; he had that quality that fascinates children but frightens them too, that makes them pause, step back, stare. She thought of the times when he'd gone to visit a friend, or his mother, and had stayed away for days or weeks. Not unusual in itself; his habits were such to make an affair easily disguised. She tried to imagine the woman's face, her neck, her hands, but she was unimaginable. At the same time she was an overwhelming presence, a body without a body that lay entwined around the body of the soft-skinned man in the bed beside her.

'What is it?' he whispered, when he woke in the night to find Hortense sitting on the edge of the bed, shivering with cold.

'Nothing,' she said, and he rolled over among the blankets and returned to sleep. As if 'nothing' did not have its own weight, its own breadth, its own depth.

It was years later that she built the bonfire in the courtyard and burnt his dead mother's belongings. She hauled them from the room in their apartment that he had set aside after his mother's death – a shrine of a room containing, among other things, drawers of clothing that smelt of camphor, a small white plaster cat, a stack of wicker baskets, newspapers, and three small wooden boxes in which lay the baby teeth of her children, Paul, Marie and Rose. Hortense imagined her mother-in-law during her long idle days in the mansion where she'd lived, opening the boxes and running her fingers over their precious contents, the tiny jewel-like teeth through which her children had cried, 'Mama, I want Mama!' She wondered if the teeth would burn to nothing in the fire or simply be blackened.

Of course, her mother-in-law was not the woman who had written that letter. But revenge is seldom direct. It is long and twisted like the years, long and twisted like the road that leads into the town of Aix, turning this way and that, edging the great Mont Sainte-Victoire that her husband had painted so many times, the fall of the light, the mountain's very shape, different in each painting. He once said that he did not aim to paint a likeness but a being-ness.

Were the twenty-nine portraits her being-ness? And was she merely their likeness?

She wrote until midmorning, the sun marching across the bed. I was pleased with the work; it seemed to confirm that all was well between us, that despite the signs from the very beginning – the sense of an undertow that I have described – she would see the project through.

'Let's go out,' she said, closing the laptop, its soft padded click the click of a tongue.

'But should we?' I said.

'Of course we should. I'm *starving*.' She hoisted her suitcase onto the bed and took out a grey tracksuit, her puffer jacket and the other items of overdressing that make up her outdoor assemblage.

'Rebecca said not to.'

She threaded her legs into the tracksuit. 'Are you my mother now?'

I shrugged. 'I'm just looking out for you.'

She laughed as she pulled on her socks.

'What's funny?'

With concise movements she tied her laces. 'The irony of *you* looking out for *me*. By the end of your life you could scarcely look out for yourself. You were a drunk. Your son had to hire a companion to help you pee.'

We went downstairs in the tiny lift. She put on a blue surgical mask from a packet she'd bought at a service station on the way from Aix the previous day. At the door of the hotel she turned and said, 'I suppose you wore a mask back then, in the time of the Spanish flu.'

I didn't answer. After all, it was not a question, and I was feeling stung by her earlier comment. She had no way of knowing the magnificence of the years that had come in a rush at the end of my life, nor the magnificence of that companion. I'd begun to tell her about it once. We were in Aix; she sat at the kitchen table studying a photo of me as an old woman. I did not look happy in the photo, I am the first to admit that, yet there was a spark in my eyes, and I began to speak to her about this spark, about the strange vitality that I came to experience at the end of my life. But she talked over me, saying that I'd aged badly and looked broken. She'd made up her mind – a fatal flaw in a writer, I thought, but what did I know?

Through the open door of the hotel lobby came the smell of the river and the dark earth. The same dark earth upon which I had roamed for my seventy-two years, and that had held me to it for a hundred more.

I breathed.

When we'd first flown into Paris from Sydney, weeks before, the writer had hired a car at de Gaulle Airport and we'd driven straight to Aix, skirting the city, sticking to freeways, passing clusters of high-rises and industrial lowlands. Now I realised that, hermetically sealed in a plane and then a car, I hadn't been able to truly smell the air of Paris. Even when we'd arrived from Aix the previous evening, dropping the hire car on the outskirts of the city and coming the rest of the way by taxi, I'd scarcely been able to draw a breath before I'd found myself in the lobby.

With the open door before me now I bounded out ahead of her, the cold air in my lungs and the smooth cobblestones beneath my feet.

I made for the river. I saw rats, who stared at me, shivering. I stared back at them, and their shivering stilled; things had not changed for rats.

In the streets, people were wary of one another in that understated way of Parisians, a way that settles about the nose and mouth. Of course, at any time there are a million reasons to be wary. The streets of Paris had never been *friendly*, in my recollection, but in them I'd felt free. Free to walk with a disgruntled step, and nobody thought the worse of you – at least not strangers. My husband's friends, they were another matter. That day people moved with a sense of hesitation, as if they didn't quite know what to do next. And then they did the next thing: they crossed the street, they went into a patisserie, they read a message on their phone. Time was newly partitioned, as if the virus, its mere existence, had cut into it, and people were only now aware of time's usual seamlessness.

Aside from the rats – who quivered and stared and stared and quivered then grew so marvellously still – apart from the rats, nobody noticed me; I was as invisible as the virus. I eavesdropped on conversations, though I could make little sense of the language. A *merci beaucoup* here, a *je suis désolé* there. Anything more complex and I drew a blank. I supposed the writer was to blame; I was living, after all, in her mind. This was how it had been ever since I'd appeared in the doorway of her study – more noticeable the moment I'd set foot in France and was once again surrounded by the French language, my mother tongue.

The city was a bombed landscape of my past life. And yet I moved along its streets with a quick light step that day with the writer, my heart beating with what felt like hope.

Hope for what? you might ask.

Hope for nothing, is all I can answer; it was simply hope.

The rhythm of the language, if not its meaning, still struck me to my depths; it was there in my every step, as the people around me carried on their conversations;

it was there in the swing of my hips and in the way my fingertips raked the soft air; it was there in the beat of my heart, a robust heart to which all my contradictions gather for sustenance.

Some glittering padlocks attached to a lamppost on a bridge caught my attention. People crossed without taking the slightest notice of the padlocks. Only the sun noticed – it looked and looked – but then the sun notices everything.

The writer followed behind me. Every now and then I turned to check that she was still there. She lagged, as I had lagged on our walks in Aix, and I found myself coaxing her as she had coaxed me.

'Come on,' I said.

Once, I turned just in time to see her going into a café, the sun on her silver hair, which streamed out from beneath her husband's hat. I stopped and waited on the corner as an ambulance appeared, wailing, and just as quickly disappeared. People paused, looked up from their phones, then down at them again. She came out carrying a takeaway coffee and a croissant. And we continued on, me in front, she following behind, the mask beneath her chin now as she sipped the coffee and nibbled at the croissant and looked into shop windows and up at the empty sky and across at the brown belly of the river. I kept turning to check that she was there, and each time that I saw she was I felt a mixture of relief and dread that reminded me of how I'd felt, long ago, as I'd hauled my mother-in-law's possessions to the bonfire.

I remembered striking the match. It was a clear day, the smoke rising lazily. My husband came running. He was so angry he couldn't speak, just eyed me with a shimmering rage. Suddenly he looked down and, cowering, began slapping at his trousers where sparks had landed. And I laughed, turning my face to the sky with its plume of smoke.

I was always on the alert for some weakness in him. I remember once standing next to him at the edge of a steep drop in Switzerland and noticing the pale plane of fear creeping over his face, for he had long been frightened of heights. Another time we were walking by the river in Paris when a dog ran towards us, barking, and my husband, usually practised at keeping his fear of dogs hidden, had darted behind me with an expression of terror. Not that I wanted to use these weaknesses against him; I had no plan or scheme. I simply wanted to thread them together, one after the other, to fumble over them like beads in a rosary.

I came close to Notre-Dame, the river between me and the church. I held on to an iron fence at the edge of the street; I don't know if it was because of the cold or the long walk, but I felt faint. Without a body, exertions are still felt; during the war, soldiers who'd returned injured from the front would cry out that a missing limb was cold or hurt, or was simply *still there*. I forgot about the writer, forgot to check that she was still there. I looked across to the burnt church, to the space in the sky above it where the spire should have been.

It was here, in Paris, that I heard that my husband was dying. I was at my dressmaker's, not far from where I stood that day – although the exact location of her apartment I could not be sure of; my mind is mired in the mind of the writer; I am not purely myself. The dressmaker – who was dear to me in a way I will tell you about later, for it was she who became the companion of my later years – was pinning a seam on the bodice of a blue dress, the pins cold against my bare side. My son, Paul, a grown man by that time, appeared in the doorway, his face long. He never had a long face; he had a plump face, more like his father's than like mine. But this day it was long; like a nightshirt it hung.

'Papa is dying.'

The dressmaker stopped pinning the seam. She drew back.

'Finish it,' I said, my voice low and calm.

Because why not finish what had been started? Was I expected to run, screaming, into the street, half naked and stuck with pins? I was and am a practical person. A bookbinder must be, to make the stitches straight and firm, to make a space to hold a story, a space to hold a whole world; it is not done out of love but out of respect, which can be truer than love.

My son left, and my dressmaker finished pinning the seam, and through the window the bells of Notre-Dame began to ring, and the light faded, and it was the next day, and still the bells rang. It was a long seam, running through the whole of my life.

By the time I reached Aix he was already dead. The room smelt of olives. He lay looking up at the ceiling, his eyes closed. But still he could see; of course he could. His eyes were shut for most of his life; even when they were open, they were shut. How else do any of us really see?

In Paris, I let go of the fence and turned, remembering the writer. A row of buildings, a woman walking a dog, a man looking at some coins in his palm, two teenagers ambling by, giggling. I could not see her. She'd taken her attention from me, I'd taken mine from her, and now she was gone. To my surprise I felt no fear, but rather a strange exhilaration, such as a deep-sea diver might feel when entering the water, knowing that their very breath may run short.

There. In a shop window, just across the street. The aquiline nose, the silver hair, the almost-sad eyes looking out from below the hat; she was speaking to a woman over a counter. The woman nodded in response. Above the door of the shop were the words *Shakespeare and Company*. And I remembered that I used to pass this shop years ago, a shop that sold books written in English.

I went in. The dusty, fresh smell of books, a smell that in my bookbinding days made me think of a field where the grass is living in some parts, dying in others. I sidled up to the writer.

'I adore her other books,' she was saying.

'Me too,' said the woman, who was small with dark hair parted sharply to one side. 'Especially her novel *Crudo*.' She sounded Australian to me, her accent like the writer's, flattened and slow.

'I'll take it,' the writer said. It was then that I noticed she was holding a book. Its cover featured an image of a man's face partially buried in earth. The book was titled *Funny Weather: Art in an emergency.*

'I'm sorry, but that's actually our advance copy. I can't sell it. The book's not out for a few weeks,' the woman said.

'I won't be here in a few weeks,' the writer said.

'I hope *I'm* not here in a few weeks,' the woman said.

'Are you flying back to Melbourne?'

'Yes.' The woman hesitated, glanced down at the counter, her fringe falling over her face. She flicked it aside and looked back at the writer. 'My partner is French, and she has to get a visa. Hopefully she can come with me.' She took a breath. 'The shop is closing tomorrow. Everything is closing. I suppose you know that.'

'I heard. It's almost a week until my flight.' The writer stared at the book.

'Tell you what, why don't you take it?'

'Really?'

'Yes, really.'

The writer reached into her bag, but the woman held up her hand.

'No payment necessary. Anyway, as I said, I can't sell an advance copy.'

'That's kind of you.' They both studied the almost-buried face on the cover of the book. There was nobody else in the shop; all was quiet and still.

'I think art is what we need now,' the woman said.

Outside, the writer said, 'Where were you?'

'I was here. Looking at the church,' I said. If she hadn't been aware of my presence in the shop, I wasn't about to point it out now.

I have noticed that I never lie to her. But nor do I tell her the whole truth.

She looked over the river towards Notre-Dame, yellowish in the sun, and stood for some time studying its scaffolded sides, its poor, broken back and the space above where its spire should be. And then she turned to me, and I thought she might ask who I'd lit the candle for, long ago, just as she had asked the night before. I wondered how I might answer, for I still couldn't make out the person's face, yet I knew that it was there, in my memory, as one knows in the dark of the night that the sun still shines somewhere in the world.

But she said, 'Let's get back to the hotel.'

She spent the next day in the room, lying on the bed reading the book she'd been given at Shakespeare and Company. She pulled it into the bed with her as if it were living and she needed to provide it with warmth and rest. She'd read for a while, then thrust the book aside and lie staring at the ceiling. At one point she picked up the phone and ordered a meal from room service, and after the meal arrived and she'd eaten it she resumed her reading. It was the first day, in all my days with her, apart from the days of travel, that she didn't write. Her laptop was on the bedside table, closed like a fist.

In Aix, whenever she had spent time reading, it was usually the large hardback titled *Madame Cezanne* that she reached for. The book had on its cover a reproduction of the portrait *Madame Cezanne in a Red Armchair*, the very painting I had found myself standing before when I awoke from my hundred years of sleep. She would pore over the pages of that book, underlining, writing in the margins, or simply staring at its cover, at the woman in the portrait who was me and not me, the silent woman forever on the verge of speech. Other times she reached for the thick biography of my husband, unsurprisingly titled *Cezanne*, or the book about the wives of Cezanne, Monet and Rodin, *Hidden in the Shadow of the Master*.

But there was another book that she read in Aix that wasn't about my husband or me at all. Titled *The Poetics of Space*, she sought it out on the nights when she couldn't sleep, the nights when she sat up, appearing troubled. On such nights she seemed far from me.

That day in the hotel, she kept the shawl close. She drew it to her as she read, as she lay staring at the ceiling. Sometimes she held it to her cheek as a child might hold a comforter while sucking their thumb; once she flung it onto the floor and lay staring at it.

Finally, as night fell, she opened her laptop and watched news of the pandemic. There were images of ambulances with sirens flashing, and patients hooked up to respirators, and tents serving as makeshift hospitals. Graphs showed the number of cases, the number of deaths. Her eyes filled with tears. 'What a fucking shit fight,' she said, sniffing.

Later, Rebecca phoned.

'I stayed in my room all day,' the writer told her.

'That's safe at least.'

'I felt too despondent to go out.'

'About the pandemic?'

'Yes. And about my command of the language. I mean, I have no command, even the basics. Just buying a croissant, it's like begging.'

'But you went to those classes at Alliance Française last year.'

'I missed most of them.'

'Mum, you're hopeless.'

'I used to lie in the bath instead of going to class. I just felt exhausted. It was still not quite a year.'

'I'm sorry. I forget it was so much harder for you, missing him every day.'

'It's okay. Anyway, I'm not sure about the book. I thought I could pull it off, but now … It's not just that I'm writing from the point of view of a French woman, and I can't bloody speak French – though what an idiot I was to think I could pull that off.'

'"It's all in the way it's done." You said that.'

'I know I *said* that. But everything's changed now. People are dying, or rushing to get across borders – all sorts of things are happening. And the book just seems … an extravagance.'

'Is Hortense still with you?'

'Yes. But she's distant.'

'Distant how?'

'Like she's off in a corner.'

'She might be waiting.'

'Waiting for what?'

'For you.'

The writer laughed shortly. 'We sound crazy, you know.'

'All my life my mother has had characters living in her head.'

'No wonder you became a psychologist.'

'No wonder.'

It is the next morning. *This* morning. The one where the writer and I stand at the window; there she is beside me, wearing an oversized T-shirt, hands on her narrow hips, the sun shining on the lines around her eyes and mouth. Just beyond her is the crack in the window with the air going in and out, in and out.

And I am filled with a glittering desire.

The sun shines on the scaffolded side of Notre-Dame and the brown river, the river I was walking beside long ago when I stopped and stared at a rat and it stared back at me and became still, truly still, inside itself; a huge achievement, to still the life of another without killing it. The sun also lights the cheeks of the child who walks ahead of the two women, and now the child starts to run, accelerating at an astonishing rate, like a jaguar on a plain. The women appear startled; they make an effort to catch up, but still they are walking, walking, and the child is running, running, speed lifting the dark hair that the light touches, as it touches the church and the river and the cobblestones.

And here is the mechanical wail, which I have already mentioned, and which, of course, is the wail of an ambulance: a terrible, inconsolable cry, the cry of this new world. The vehicle itself comes into view now, square-bottomed and pale, hurtling around the corner near the burnt church – just as the child reaches the kerb and flies out into the street.

What is the child running from, or to? Perhaps it is neither. Perhaps the child merely runs; perhaps running is what the child *is*.

The screech of tyres, and the tiny, tiny thud, an insect-heartbeat of a thud; can anyone say they hear it, really, the moment of impact, the moment it happens, the moment it all comes together, the whole drawn-out choreography of that instant?

The women are running – too late but running – making their way in the story they will from now on be tangled in, knotted by, the story that begins here, on this sunlit street. Their masks are askew, their mouths caverns as they scream; the bags of groceries lie on the cobblestones like the strokes of a painting: some greenery, a stick of bread, carrots. The screams reach the window where the writer and I stand. Muffled by distance and the glass, they are terrifying in their smallness.

The women kneel either side of the child. They have stopped screaming, and their mouths form words, inaudible from this distance. The paramedics are out of the ambulance, and like birds they hover. A stretcher is brought – far too long. It looks like a landing strip, and the writer cannot bear it anymore. She leaves the window, goes to the bed and lies curled on her side, knees up to her chest, and sobs quietly as the sun rises higher, and the ambulance wails off with the child and the two women inside.

I sit beside her as the sun shifts across the bed. She opens her eyes, closes them. There is something about sitting for long periods in stillness – and my husband insisted on stillness; he stood and threw his arms in the air and exclaimed that the world was against him if I so much as scratched my ear – there is something that creeps over you and through you, like a vine, something living and doomed, a thing that makes you aware that life is less seamless than you'd imagined, that it is a series of discrete moments, each separated from the next, each living its own desire.

She has abandoned the book. I know this.

Yet here I sit, watching her eyelashes in the sun, greyish like dirty snow. Watching her as she pulls the doona close and kicks one leg free. It is not through pity that I sit; it is not through a feeling of obligation, such as I felt when I sat for my husband: the obligation of a muse, the obligation of a wife.

She has lost interest in me. But I grow more interested in her.

Is she *my* subject?

Around midday she reaches for the hotel phone and orders food, then goes to the bathroom and returns, naked. Sitting on the bed, the shawl around her shoulders, she opens the laptop and begins to write. I move towards her, but there is a barrier between us; I cannot go to her, cannot stand at her shoulder and see the words that flow from her fingers. But more than ever I long to see them; it is the longing of a new love, such as I had for my husband, and he had for me, in the first months after we met, when all he could do was stare at my face. Even when he was not sketching or painting it he stared at my face, and when we made love he stared at my face, as he moved above me and I felt the world open below, a pit of wonder.

The meal arrives. She goes to the window with a bowl and stands there eating, looking out, while I watch the silver laptop on the bed, its contents forbidden to me, like the contents of the little wooden box she took from her bedside drawer in Bondi. *It's nothing to do with you.*

After lunch she continues to write. Hours pass, the light fades and I realise that, like yesterday, she will not be going out. She is on what she calls 'a roll', her fingers racing across the keyboard. She pauses every now and then to stare at the floor, at the window, at the bed; she is seeing inside herself.

Night comes, and still she writes. Her cheeks droop. She takes sips of water from a glass. Like yesterday, she has had one meal in the day.

At last, somewhere near midnight, she closes the laptop and lies back and falls into a deep, exhausted sleep.

And I sit, through the hours until dawn, watching her lined face, watching the rise and fall of her chest and the way she turns in her sleep from her side to her back to her other side with an indolence that is missing from her waking hours, as if a solution to any ill need only be sought in sleep.

At sunrise I stand at the window, watching the place in the street where the child was hit. There is no mark of blood on the cobblestones, no mark from the screech of tyres. A couple of people walk by as if nothing has happened, and as far as they know nothing *has* happened. The world is full of a lack of proof.

She lies on her side, one arm cradling her head, the laptop close to her bare spine. It is dimly grey, like an oyster. On impulse I go to it – nothing stops me. With a handless hand I lift its lid; I have learnt a new skill. I read through the morning, as the room grows ever brighter, and she sleeps on, giving my attention to the words she wrote after the child was hit. There is no proof on the cobblestones. But there is proof on the page.

PART II

PART II

DEAR REBECCA,

Something happened here in this room. Or, rather, it didn't happen in this room, but I witnessed it from this room.

To witness an event. Sometimes the place you witness it from seems as relevant as the event itself.

It happened just this morning. And now I feel so tired. I think it is grief – a deep, old grief brought to the surface by what I just saw.

A child was run over. A child flew out into the street and was hit by an ambulance. An *ambulance*. Yes. The irony is not lost on me, the witness, and I'm sure it is not lost on the paramedics; and certainly it is not lost on the two women who were walking with the child, who I think are the parents. But it is lost on the sky and on the cobblestones and on the burnt church of Notre-Dame; it is lost on the scene itself.

What I witnessed has brought me to this place, here, finally. I don't mean to this room. I mean to this place inside myself, a place I have been moving towards for a long time, Rebecca, perhaps for years, and especially these past weeks in France.

You probably wonder why I have kept silent all these years. Silence is seen as a weakness these days, a means of denying the true life of the self, one's own history, and of course in some sense this is true. But it assumes that words are always up to the task, and I do not believe that they are. It might surprise you that I do not put all my trust in words. I am wary of them. Words are wild animals; I keep a respectful distance. I do not hunt them; I let them come to me.

There have been times when you have drawn close to the story I am about to tell you. When we were talking the other night, just a few weeks ago – my last night in Sydney – I thought you'd stumbled on it, and I wondered if the right words might come at last.

As we sat on the deck and you poured the wine, I listened to the ocean whispering up the broad Bondi streets. I thought of Lucas and how tired he'd been earlier, falling asleep even as I read to him. You were like that in your first year at school, exhausted by the long days. I remember once, you fell asleep while still eating your dinner. These memories are what led me to mention Malcolm, I think, though you'd agree we each bring the subject around to him pretty much as often as we can. This is more than comfort; it is a means of keeping his heart beating between us, that heart that stopped so suddenly. I often imagine him on that day, at work, in his office, slumping onto his keyboard. It is in the moment of death that he springs to life, that he seems to protest, *How can this happen to me?*

So he was on my mind when you saw the possum, and I told you about our experience with the possum piper. I'm sorry I brought up the baby possums – you looked horrified. I suppose it was the idea of the trapped baby possums that made me say what I said next.

No, I don't suppose. I'm sure it was.

'You know I left your father, once.'

You said nothing at first, just kept your soft gaze on me, the kind of gaze that cuts through. A sharp gaze is useless; a sharp gaze gives advance warning; it is softness that uncovers things.

And I grew nervous then. As I felt you edging closer to the story that has existed all these years somewhere beyond me, living its own life. It is unsettling to know that your life has a trajectory apart from itself.

'How come you never told me?' you said, but before I could begin to reply, you cocked your head to the side and, with a look of calm alarm – contradiction is at home in the very muscles of a mother's face – you said, 'Is that Lucas?' and got up and went inside to check on your sleeping boy.

I remained on the deck, alone, the blood surging in my neck as if I had just stepped back from a precipice.

Later, when we moved back inside, and Francis rang and you went into the lounge room to talk to him, I took teacups from the shelf and milk from the fridge and turned over in my mind the exchange we'd had on the deck. How I'd told you that, once, I'd left your father; how you'd begun to question me about it but had then, suddenly, gone inside to check on Lucas.

And it seems to me now, as I write in this room on the other side of the world, beside the burnt church of Notre-Dame, at the beginning of a pandemic which will last who knows how long, that Lucas holds all of your hopes and mine beneath his gently closed lids.

She stirs. Sits up. And I retreat to the window. I do not want her to know that I am reading her story. I'm not sure why. I only know that I feel a new distance from her – a distance that, oddly, draws me close. Watching her is like watching the sea from a plane: there is the glinting surface, the shadows of clouds and the amorphous shape of the currents beneath.

She blinks at the open laptop, then reaches out and closes it.

Later she orders food from room service and continues to write, and I remain at the window. I long to stand at her shoulder, but I can't; there is an ocean between us.

All day, the mouse-like shuffle of her fingers on the keyboard, a delivered meal, dirty crockery. Intermittently she leaves the bed and paces back and forth, or goes to the window to look out, or to her suitcase to pick out an item of clothing that she throws on, then later throws off. The discarded garments form an archipelago across the white carpet.

After it has grown dark, Rebecca calls.
 'Darling.'
 'Mum. How are you?'
 'Good.'
 'You look tired.'
 'I've been writing.'
 'Great.'
 'It's ... not the book. It's something new.'
 'Oh? What?'
 'I can't talk about it yet – you know how it goes. I have to let it find its feet.' She takes a breath, and her tone shifts. 'So, how are you and Francis? And Lucas?'
 'We're fine. Trying to get our heads around the prospect of homeschooling. It hasn't come to that yet, but there's talk. Mum, you look ... terrible. Are you okay?'
 'I'm fine. I wrote all day. I may have forgotten to eat.'
 'I wish Dad was there with you.'
 'Oh, he'd hate Paris with everything closed. I walked past the Musée d'Orsay the other day, all shuttered and gloomy. It's so depressing. It's as if art is being – muzzled somehow. I did manage to visit Shakespeare and Co before it closed. Came away with a book called *Funny Weather: Art in an emergency*.'

'Prescient title.'

'Isn't it. It's about the lives of various artists. One is Georgia O'Keeffe. You know, when Georgia's husband died, the coffin she chose for him had pink satin lining, and the night before his funeral she ripped it out and replaced it with white linen. She sewed it herself. Somehow, I can't get this image out of my mind. Her husband, Alfred Stieglitz, had been having a relationship with another woman. It just seems genius to me – to destroy the space where his body would lie, and then remake it, reclaim it.'

'Did Dad have an affair? Is that why you left him?' Rebecca asks.

'What?' The writer gives a little laugh. 'No, Bec, it was nothing like that.'

After the phone call the writer turns off the lamp and lies for a long time, as the shifting lights from the cars in the street sweep through the room. Just as her eyelids grow heavy, she rouses herself, sits up and, reaching for the laptop, proceeds to write for some hours, every now and then sneezing and drawing the shawl close.

Finally, she sleeps, and I go to the laptop. Once again, I lift its lid and read as the night spreads itself beyond me, the low hum of the traffic outside punctuated now and then by the wail of an ambulance: sometimes close, sometimes far off.

This is the story of how you came to be, Rebecca. It is not a story about you, but it leads to you; it points to you. I suppose that is true of all stories, that they point to a thing beyond themselves.

This story starts with a woman walking on a beach. The woman is me, yet she is not me. In order to place ourselves in the past it is necessary to make strangers of ourselves. I will call her Georgia, after Georgia O'Keeffe, who ripped the lining from her husband's coffin the night before his funeral. The name is apt.

The year is 1990 and Georgia, who was – what? – thirty-six years old then, walks south along Coogee Beach in Sydney, the sand so cold it numbs her feet. The sea lies glassy and innocuous; it's always like this just before the sun. She turns at the end of the beach near the sea pool just as the sun breaks the horizon, and shadows appear on the water, its surface shattering with dark and light.

She makes her way to the café at the edge of the beach. Outside, she brushes the sand from her feet and slips on the shoes she has carried in her bag.

Inside, she finds a corner table, orders a flat white and takes her notebook from her bag. Georgia works for a magazine in Surry Hills. She comes to this café every morning to write in her notebook before going to work; a quiet, uninterrupted start to her day with words. She writes articles and reviews of art shows; theatre; films; sometimes fashion, about which she knows little; and gardening, about which she knows even less. At the magazine she's valued for her versatility and her ability to make any topic seem like *her* topic. It's all in the tone and the rhythm, Georgia thinks; if these are right, it almost doesn't matter what she says.

In the first draft of an article, she writes by feel and lets anything in – that is, anything that glows, that holds a certain attraction. Later, much is discarded. But here in the café she finds herself reading over those discarded lines: a description of a man at a bus stop fumbling in his pocket for change, a child screaming in a car, the smell of an orange. The lines are by no means astonishing or beautiful, and it is perhaps for this reason that she is drawn to them; it's as if they have not lived up to some potential, as if they have fallen short.

She has no interest, yet, in writing fiction. She does not know that these discarded lines are leading her there.

The light shifts and she looks up as someone enters the café. It's Malcolm, her husband. She registers this with a little shock in her throat. He wears corduroy trousers and a blue jacket, his face stubbled with short growth, and his dark hair is glossy, longer than she remembers it, curling against his neck. She hasn't seen him in four months.

She puts down her pen.

'Georgia.' He uses the name I've just chosen for her, and it places an aura of reality over the scene. A character, when they enter a story, must be willing to drop their preconceptions of what the story is. Malcolm is willing.

He walks towards her with a studied precision that isn't natural to him. Is it to do with his surprise at seeing her? No. His coming to this café at this time of day means he expects to see her. Her routine is well known to him. An early morning walk on the beach, and then coffee at a corner table while she writes. It's been her routine since before they met four years ago, at the birthday party of a mutual friend, playing bocce on the headland at Clovelly, both of them novices, the ocean roaring behind them. They'd laughed at one another's inaccurate attempts to hit the jack while the sea glistened darkly behind them. They'd both known that sea was their future – they'd talked about it weeks later, the first time they went to bed together: how their future had spread itself behind them on that first day, glistening and alive.

He reaches the table, looks at the chair opposite hers but doesn't sit; he looks at it as if he isn't sure it's a chair.

'It's your father,' he says.

The last thing she expects to hear. Her father doesn't exist during these mornings in the café, at least not up close. He's somewhere in the background, deep in a sea like the one that spread itself behind her and Malcolm on that first day, a sea that feeds her words but seldom reveals a source, a sea that remains incognito as she writes.

Now, her father rises to the surface. There he is, at the house on the farm near Brisbane where she grew up, and where he still lives, with her mother, sitting on the verandah reading *The Queensland Times*, his glasses crookedly held together across their broken bridge with sticky tape. A child of the depression, he prides himself on making do.

'He's had a stroke. Your mother called. She couldn't get you, so she called me.'

She imagines her father falling from the chair, his glasses clattering to the ground and breaking again across the bridge. Is it a metaphor for life, that we break in the places where we are already broken? The newspaper settles on the boards of the verandah, boards with wide gaps through which, when she was a child, she'd watched a succession of newborn pups feed and squirm against their cattle dog mother.

'Where is he?'

'In hospital. In Brisbane.'

Brisbane. An hour and a half from the farm. A city dissected by a muddy river and bordered by a ragged line of hills.

'Which hospital?'

'The Royal. You have to go up there, Georgia. It's … your mother said it's serious.'

A stroke. The stroke of a pen. Something ruled out. A heart attack was preferable. You could fight an attack. But a stroke … She knows this logic has nothing to do with science; it has to do with words.

'Do you want me to book you a flight?'

'No, I can do it.' She shoves the notebook into her bag, stands, bumps against the edge of the table, vaguely registering pain in her thigh, and makes her way outside. The sunlight is warm on her head.

He follows and stands close. His eyes are red, with fine sprays of veins in their whites, and she realises that he's been crying.

He loves my father. She registers this as if it is something new, but it isn't; it's the context that's new. In two months she will apply for a divorce; she phoned Malcolm recently and told him so. Her solicitor will send him the papers.

At uni her friends said they would never marry, 'because a piece of paper means nothing'. But a piece of paper possesses mysterious powers, far beyond the words that are written on it; Georgia knows this.

'I'll fly to Brisbane with you,' Malcolm says, as she watches the sea beyond him flopping lazily onto the beach. The Coogee surf is renowned for being deceptive. She's been fooled by it herself, dragged across the sandy bottom by even the smallest wave, coming up spluttering, once with a grazed elbow and knee, another time with half a beach's worth of sand through her hair. Recently, a traveller dived into a wave at Coogee, hit a sand bar and was paralysed from the neck down. Sometimes there are helicopter rescues off the cliffs to the north of the beach, the helicopter hovering low and clumsy for as long as it dares, pummelling the shrubs at the cliff's edge, the chugging of its engine fanning out across suburbs.

'I'm okay to go alone,' she says, studying the weave and cut of his jacket, the way it sits across his shoulders. A jacket, she remembers suddenly, that she gave him for his birthday two years ago. And now her tears come, not for her father – those will come later – but for this: what was given in another time, a time of love, has gone on existing regardless.

In Paris, she writes all through the next day, her chin pulled close to her chest, her lips pointed in concentration. As night falls, she leaves the laptop and goes to the corner of the room where some books lie and picks out *The Poetics of Space*, the book she read on sleepless nights in Aix.

She sits on the edge of the bed and reads for some time, and then she turns out the light and remains sitting, looking around the room, making a slow, careful study of its muted walls and the long shadow that falls across the bed, the shadow that I thought, on our first night in the hotel, was the shadow of the spire of Notre-Dame, until I remembered there was no longer a spire, that the spire has fallen in.

After a while she opens the laptop and goes on writing through the long hours of the night. As morning comes, I notice that her skin glows strangely, and that her eyes are red-rimmed. She closes the laptop and goes to the bathroom. I hear the toilet flush, the splash of water in the basin. And when she comes back to the room, everything is different.

Or rather, this is the moment that I *know* everything is different.

She begins to cough, her back rounding forward. I can see the outline of her ribs. She coughs and coughs, and when it finally ends she sits on the carpet, legs akimbo.

'You're sick,' I say.

She opens her mouth as if to answer but begins to cough again, and I notice that she is sweating, her hair stuck to her forehead. Like a wounded insect she crawls to the bed and gets in, and with a trembling hand takes a glass of water from the bedside table and sips, then reaches for the hotel phone and calls reception, speaking for a short time, listening, speaking again, the conversation finding its rhythm.

I have a cough. And a fever. I need to be tested. Can you arrange it? Is there a doctor? A clinic? That's kind. Of course I will stay in my room. Can you send up some soup? Left at the door? And sheets, at the door. I will change the bed myself.

And now, in the middle of the day, she sleeps. Dressed in tracksuit, socks and beanie, as if ready to go outside. But she stays inside, the doona pulled high, her breath short, her cheeks bright.

And I continue to read the story written over the past few days, the story that is for Rebecca.

For what else am I to do? I cannot stop what has begun.

This is the part where I go to see my father when he is dying. As you know, he died the year before you were born. But here, I must pause to tell you the reason I am writing this to you. I mean, the reason I am *writing* it, rather than telling it to you when I come home, as I promised I would.

Writing is different from talking. There is more space in it, and this is a story that needs space; a story that has been crammed inside me, breathless, for most of my life; a story that I cannot tell you by talking. At least, not in a way that tells it right. I came to know this only yesterday, as I watched the two women kneel either side of the child in the street.

Georgia sits in the taxi on the way to the hospital. The muddy smell of Brisbane. Sydney smells of brightness and light, but Brisbane is muddy, a kind of interior.

The cab heads along Kingsford Smith Drive, the long arm of the river to her left. She went to uni in Brisbane, moving from the farm straight after high school. Her last year of school had been hard, a year spent living outside of her own body. The three years in Brisbane, near the muddy river, had brought her back to herself.

The taxi passes through Auchenflower, with its steep, lush hills and its verandahs like drooping eyelids. She'd lived in a tiny flat on her own at the bottom of one of these streets. Her uni friends had all lived in share houses, or at home, but she'd wanted to be on her own. She remembers her father kneeling on the floor of the kitchen of her flat, holding a toothbrush, cleaning the grout between the tiles so that she could get her bond back. She can't remember her mother being there, but she supposes she was. She just has this image of her father.

The father who has had a stroke. Will he be conscious when she arrives at the hospital? Will he be able to speak?

Her father kneeling on the tiles had not spoken. He'd been too intent on doing a good job. On cleaning the grout so that she could get her bond back, so that she could move to Sydney the following month to take up a job as a cadet journalist, her first real job. *We're proud of you, Georgia*, he might have said as he knelt on those tiles. But she is sure that he did not say this – at least, she is sure that he did not use the word 'proud'. It didn't matter that she'd done well at uni, or that she'd landed a good job in a field where it was hard to land a job at all. She'd forfeited the right to words such as 'proud' in year eleven. A line had been drawn then, and it would not have occurred to her father to cross it.

The hospital comes into view, its many layers against the blue sky; it's like a cruise liner.

She pays the driver and thanks him, but does not smile. People are circumspect about smiling at strangers in this city. It seems a bit forward or impolite to do so before at least having had a conversation, and as they have not exchanged a word more than is necessary – her destination, the final price, thank you – her face, and his, remain impassive.

She goes up in the lift and follows the signs to the ward. Walking along a corridor, she notices a woman sitting on a chair at the other end, a woman she knows is her mother, even though she can't see her very well because of the distance of this corridor; it is unusually long, stretched in years. *What makes this woman at the end of the corridor my mother?* thinks Georgia. *What is a mother when you are making her up?*

Georgia walks, her shoes slapping against the shining floor. Everything about this walk along the corridor, which has no windows to the outside world – an interior sheltered from the true light of day – everything about it is reflected. And now Georgia is close enough to the woman to make her out, or at least parts of her.

Her hands, her mother's hands, come into focus, clutching one another like children just out of a bath. These hands are more than a mother's hands; they are human hands.

But still, it's not enough to have human hands with freckles and crooked nails and a worn part on the forefinger, from sewing, on a mother, on the idea of a mother. She's still a kind of cliché. Let her speak.

'Georgia,' her mother says.

So she, like Malcolm, is willing. Willing to go with the name that is not her name, the name that she lives by here on the page. Will anyone refuse her in this story?

Her mother inclines her head towards a pair of white swing doors, and something in the angle of the head, the jut of the jaw, says that she will not do Georgia's bidding, after all; she will do her own bidding.

'Georgia is in there with him now,' her mother says.

'But *I'm* Georgia.' She tries to sound sure.

'Yes, of course.' Her mother waves a freckled hand, as if there is no contradiction. 'You are in there with him now.'

Georgia steps towards the white swing doors, just as a nurse bursts through them, her uniform fragile and crisp as the wings of a butterfly.

'How is he?' asks Georgia.

'He's dead,' says the nurse, and with an air of efficiency pads off down the corridor, her buttocks jumping up and down beneath her uniform.

Georgia turns to her mother.

'Do I know he's dead?'

'Of course you know he's dead!' Her mother almost smiles. 'You were a clever child. I never had to help you with your homework. Not once.'

The man on the bed is not her father. She sees this as soon as she enters the room, even though he has her father's high-bridged nose and streaks of grey at the temples and his dimpled chin. The match is close. Close enough for Georgia to say, inside herself, this is my father, the father of me, Georgia, who lives in a story that pours from a writer's

hands into a laptop in a hotel in the centre of Paris, outside
the window of which, due to a highly contagious virus,
there are few people in the streets; outside the window of
which is a scaffolded, burnt church and the intermittent
wail of ambulances and a sense that life has been put on
hold, the pump of blood in veins and air in lungs paused.

Stay home. Stop the spread. She is still trying to get her
head around it; the whole world is trying to get its head
around it: this need to stay still, to do nothing, to play dead.

Georgia takes her father's hand. Cold as the lifeless cat
she once found at the side of the road on her way home
from school, in her childhood – her clever childhood.

'Dad, it's Georgia,' she says. The set of his mouth
is loose, easy, in a way of seeming convinced. A tight
mouth – now that would appear unconvinced. She is
glad she noticed this about his mouth, glad that she has
reached this conclusion, that he is convinced.

'Dad,' she says again, though she doesn't speak aloud
this time, but says the word inside herself; language is
bigger inside. 'Dad, remember how you cleaned the
kitchen floor when I moved out of the flat in Auchenflower
when I finished university? So that I could get my bond
back? I was moving to Sydney. For my first job. You
cleaned the grout with a toothbrush. A *toothbrush.* Down
on your hands and knees.'

His hair is smoothed over his forehead in a way he
would not tolerate in life. In life he pushed his hair back,

running his hand through it as he spoke, as he thought, as he laughed. A habit. In death there are new habits. The habit of stillness, the habit of silence, the habit of giving up.

'There's another day I remember, Dad,' she goes on, and her voice, inside herself, is far off. She has to run, inside herself, to catch up. 'A day in year eleven. It was some years before you knelt on the tiles with the toothbrush. I walked up the road from the school bus. The sun was shining on the silky oaks near the house. I came up the stairs and inside and I said something to you and Mum, something I'd rehearsed as I'd watched the sun on those trees. I said it, and your eyes were very blue as you turned towards the phone. You called the priest. He came and sat at our kitchen table. By then the sun was gone. Mum switched on the lights and boiled the jug and made the tea and we all sat – you, Mum, the priest, me. The priest's hands were delicate. I'd never seen delicate hands on a man. You were a farmer – look, even your dead hand in mine now, it's tough as wood. The priest's hand was baby smooth as he held the cup. He said nothing and you said nothing; he looked at you and you looked at him. It was decided then.'

On the bed her father does not speak. Of course he does not speak; he's dead. But still, he speaks. Out of his convinced mouth, he says, 'Not one word of this is from my point of view.'

When Georgia comes back out into the corridor, she sees that her mother's eyes are red from crying.

'The others are waiting at home. Ingrid is cooking a roast.' Her mother sniffs and stands, straightening her skirt.

So, I have siblings, Georgia thinks, and in a rush she remembers the feel of being among them as a child: the feel of skin on skin, the feel of breath on breath, the feel of wish on wish.

How many of them are there? Does she love them? Does she know them?

It thrills her to think that she might know them. It thrills her and scares her – for fear is just another way of being thrilled.

Do they know about *it*?

When they get home, the family gathers around the kitchen table, the same table from long ago. Its legs are made of steel, and it has a pink laminex top.

The brothers and sisters sit close. They pass the salt. They eat Ingrid's roast chicken and vegetables. The meal is delicious. Her sister knows how to keep the juices in the flesh. Does she use an oven bag, Georgia wants to ask, or is the secret in the basting? Ingrid's brow is sweaty; her fringe sticks to it, and Georgia decides that Ingrid is the basting type, the type to make a meal from scratch, the type to eschew shortcuts, the type to have a veggie patch and to not colour her hair – yes, a few silvers in the fringe confirm this.

Does she have children, this sister?

A knot twists in Georgia's chest.

If the story were a straight line, it might head away from the grieving family about now, out through the window and over the paddocks, over eucalypts and wallabies and cattle tracks and roads to the coast. A straight line longs to extend into space, to find what is new.

But the story is a circle. It longs for what is old. It stays close to this table of mother, sisters, brothers, all getting stuck into a roast dinner, gravy dribbling down their chins; grief makes you ravenous. In particular, the story circles the sister with the silver in her fringe.

What did this sister know twenty years earlier, in 1970? What knowledge did she carry around beneath her not-yet-silver fringe?

The morning after, Georgia and Ingrid hang out the washing around the side of the house, the long clothesline slung on grey posts. Georgia hangs her father's work trousers, worn at the knees, smelling of horse, despite the influence of a strong detergent.

Beside her Ingrid reaches for a fistful of pegs, the sun shining on the back of her neck.

'You were older than me,' Georgia says, reaching for some pegs too.

Ingrid straightens and smiles. 'I am still.'

Georgia rummages in the basket and her hand comes out with a singlet, her father's, its armholes large and lank.

'You had a boyfriend,' she says, remembering teenaged Ingrid walking hand in hand with a boy near the woodheap. It was dusk. Georgia watched them as she collected wood-chips so her father could start the fire the next morning. Her mother had sent her – 'Gather some chips and bring them in so they're dry for morning,' her mother had said. Her mother cooked porridge in the mornings.

'It's like we live in a fairytale,' Georgia said once.

'In some ways we do,' her mother replied.

'Hello,' Georgia had said, as Ingrid and the boy made their way towards her at the woodheap, heads bowed.

They both looked up. 'Hello,' Ingrid said.

The boyfriend's eyes flashed in the dying light. And Georgia knew that he was noticing her, and she knew that noticing was different from looking, that noticing had its own inevitable momentum. She held the wood chips against her chest, the ends digging through her T-shirt and into her skin.

'I'm going in,' she said, and turned.

'I'll be in soon,' Ingrid said after her.

The boy said nothing, but she knew that he went on noticing her as she walked up the track to the house.

'I took him off you,' she says to Ingrid now, while securing the second peg on the arm of the singlet.

Ingrid laughs. 'I *gave* him to you.'

'You didn't want him?'

'You wanted him more.'

'So, he was a thing to pass back and forth?'

'He didn't mind. He thought it was Christmas.'

Georgia picks up a pair of her mother's underpants, white sagging cottontails. A shiver runs through her. Her mother was in the kitchen the day the priest came. She made the tea, ensuring that the water was properly boiled, spooning in the leaves, turning the pot once.

'She didn't stick up for me,' Georgia says, as she pegs the underpants.

'She didn't know how to,' Ingrid says.

And then she frowns. She is holding a sock in each hand. Long and black, they could belong to their mother or their father.

'That's not quite true,' Ingrid goes on. 'She thought she *was* sticking up for you. By letting it happen.'

An old sting uncoils in Georgia's throat. 'Where were you that afternoon?'

'In my room studying. You already know that.' Ingrid calmly pegs the socks, one by one. 'I was in my final year.' A slight hardness enters her voice. 'You already know that.'

'Well, you should have come *out* of your room. You should have come out of your room and *said* something.'

But Ingrid won't be drawn. She searches in the wash basket for the next item, and Georgia recognises a pattern between herself and Ingrid, a pattern that has been there since they were teenagers, a kind of dance in which they are forever approaching one another and stepping back. Ingrid pegs the last item, a handkerchief, then points to a silky oak in the creek paddock. She smiles. 'Remember we used to play under that tree.'

Two cows stand in the shade beneath the tree. They stare at Georgia and Ingrid, their tummies huge, their heads weighed with bone, as the sun shifts, and Georgia remembers how she and Ingrid would drag their dolls and some old towels to beneath this tree, spreading the towels on the ground to form the floor of a house, weighing the corners with rocks. The house had no walls or roof – these had to be imagined out of empty space.

'You should have said something.'

'I didn't know.'

'You knew.'

It is mesmerising, this dance with her sister. They are close in age and look alike, with the same wide-spaced eyes. At night, long ago, one of them would leave their bed to crawl in with the other, for they could not bear to sleep apart. Their mother used to say they were joined at the hip.

Time in the hotel room rocks like a slow ship – this way, that – and the writer's condition stays the same: no better, no worse. She shivers, and I wish I could place a cool cloth on her forehead, as my mother used to for me when I had a fever. I go into the bathroom. There are towels in damp piles on the floor. A wet cloth hangs on the side of the bath and I try to pick it up, but my hand only grasps the air.

I can lift the lid of a laptop; otherwise, I am useless.

Tonight, Rebecca calls.

'Mum, you look awful.' She sounds shocked. 'You're sick. Why didn't you tell me?'

She asks a few quick questions to which her mother gives answers in a tiny, cracked voice, and then she hangs up, promising to call back after she's spoken to the staff at the hotel.

When she does call back, her voice has changed. Its tone is efficient and reassuring, and I imagine it is a tone that she uses in her work as a psychologist. She explains that she tried to arrange for a doctor to come, but it is almost impossible to find one; there are so many sick people, and there's also the risk of spreading infection. 'And I've asked about getting you a test,' she says, 'but that's tricky too, as it would require going to a clinic, and that's also an infection risk.'

'I may not even have it,' the writer almost whispers.

'We have to assume. Anyway, the person I spoke to was really helpful. She told me how they're already bringing you soups and clean sheets and towels and ibuprofen. And they've asked me to remind you that if your condition gets worse, especially if you have difficulty in breathing, you're to call reception, and they will call an ambulance. They can arrange that. So don't worry, you're in good hands. And use your puffer when you need, of course. Remember, Dad used to say that despite your occasional asthma you were the one with the good constitution, that if one of you was to get sick it would be him and not you. And don't worry about your flight, I'm on it. I'll change it to a day when you'll be better. We'll get you home. For now, you rest. You take it day by day.'

There are many brothers, but just the one sister. Georgia has established this. The brothers are capable. They ride horses; they chop wood to feed the fire in the combustion stove. Georgia grew up with this stove. It hummed in winter and roared in summer. Its sound was always the same, but the world read it differently. In summer it was a curse to the whole house; everyone's brow was damp. In winter the family gathered near it, cups of tea in hand.

'How many brothers are there?' Georgia asks her mother, as her mother cuts pieces from a bolt of red velvet spread on the kitchen table. She is making a dress to wear to the funeral.

'Can't you count?' The scissors crunch through the fabric.

'Counting doesn't work.'

Her mother laughs. 'And you were the clever one.'

The one sister, of course, is Ingrid, who hides behind her silver-flecked fringe, who steps out from behind the fringe now and then to speak. Two nights after their father's death, Georgia and Ingrid wash up. Ingrid washing, Georgia wiping, just as they did long ago. The brothers are nowhere in sight. Washing up is the work of sisters, not brothers. Brothers chop wood, brothers ride horses, brothers string the wire in a fence.

At the sink Ingrid says, 'I went to town with Mum today.' She draws a cup from the water and puts it onto the dish rack. 'She chose Dad's coffin.'

Georgia reaches for the cup and begins to wipe it with the tea towel. She was not aware of Ingrid and her mother's trip to town.

'Where was I?' she asks. She tries to remember what she did that day, but she draws a blank.

'You were distracted.'

'Distracted by what?'

'What you're always distracted by.'

Georgia shoves the tea towel into the cup and twists it back and forth. 'You should have said something.'

'I didn't know.'

'You knew.'

'What makes you so sure?'

'We were joined at the hip.'

Ingrid has two little girls, aged eight and nine. At first, their names are beyond Georgia, but now they come into focus: matter-of-fact names. Zoe and Alice. They call her 'Aunty Georgia'; they have some claim to her.

'Aunty Georgia, why don't you have children?' asks Zoe. She is young enough to be missing her eye teeth, which makes her look ratty.

'I don't want them,' Georgia says, standing at the bench chopping celery.

'There's still time,' says Georgia's mother, who sits at the sewing machine in the corner, snipping the thread from a seam she's just sewed on the red dress.

The two girls watch Georgia closely. Georgia pauses in her chopping to shove a few pieces of celery their way.

'Don't you *like* children?' asks Zoe, chomping on the celery.

'Don't be rude,' Alice admonishes her sister, but she too eyes Georgia and waits for a reply, a circumspection to her gaze. *She is at the age where she is starting to draw away*, Georgia thinks.

'Of *course* she likes children!' her mother says from the corner.

Later, her mother leaves the room and returns with a knitted garment in her hands. Georgia is at the stove stirring a pot of stew. Her face is overheated. She takes the spoon out of the pot and steps back.

'There's too much wood on this fire,' she says.

'The brothers tend to overdo the wood when they come home,' her mother says with an edge of pride. 'Remember this?' She holds the garment towards Georgia. 'I found it in the back of my material cupboard when I was looking for the red velvet.'

Georgia's throat is suddenly dry as she recognises the shawl. Her mother knitted it for her twenty years earlier, on her sixteenth birthday. She took it with her when she went away – when she was *sent* away.

'I thought you might want it,' her mother says.

'I don't.' Georgia steps back to the stove and resumes her stirring as her mother studies the shawl, holding it up, spreading it, examining its stitches. 'I had a bit of trouble with the pattern, I remember. There was some complication I couldn't get at first. It ended up with a few mistakes.'

Georgia stirs the stew that will feed the countless brothers, her mother, Ingrid, Zoe, Alice and herself. No wonder her arm aches.

'I'll leave it in your room, in case you change your mind,' her mother says, and goes out into the hallway. Georgia, at the stove, feels the strange satisfaction of being close to a thing that burns too bright.

The shawl was around her shoulders when she signed the piece of paper, long ago: the piece of paper that said that her baby was not her baby. She cannot remember much about the room in which she signed the paper, except that it was bright with sunlight and that the baby was big inside her by then, moving in her this way, that way, as if he had a perfect right, as if there was no question that he was hers, and she was his. She cannot remember the other person in the room, but she knows there was someone, possibly a nun. She cannot even remember the piece of paper with much clarity; it was simply a piece of paper – a piece of paper that, she would come to understand much later, stood for far more than the words that were written on it. But she remembers the feel of the shawl around her shoulders as she put the pen to the paper; she remembers the weight of it, the slight prickliness of it, the warmth of it.

Through the kitchen window come the voices of Zoe and Alice, who are playing in the garden. They laugh, they shout, and now one of them begins to wail, a drawn-out cry of pain and outrage, and the other follows suit. Georgia wonders if she should go to them, but she doesn't; she stays where she is at the too-hot stove. And now she hears Ingrid's voice. 'Why can't you just leave her be,' Ingrid is saying. 'She doesn't have to do everything you ask.'

And Georgia's mind goes to a scene from long ago.

Her baby boy in her arms. The nurse brought him to her soon after he was born. Most girls weren't so lucky, the nurse said, but she could tell that Georgia wasn't the type to do anything silly, the type to scream and huddle in a corner with the baby held too tightly, or, god forbid, make a run for it down the corridor and out into the day with no plan for how to look after a baby alone, and with a fresh cut and stitches from the birth. The nurse could tell that Georgia had 'a level head'. And so she let her hold the baby, briefly, and while Georgia held him the nurse produced a tiny pair of scissors and carefully cut a lock of his dark hair for Georgia to keep. And then she took him away and Georgia was left with the lock of hair, stroking it with her fingers and wondering how her body – her poor, slashed-apart body that had just pushed him into the world – how it had been able to produce anything so soft.

Through the window Zoe – or it might be Alice, she cannot tell – screams at the top of her lungs.

'*No! No! No! No! No!*'

In Paris, the writer sleeps in fits and starts, dressed like an overenthusiastic tourist from a temperate climate who fears that any moment they might encounter snow. She coughs into the sleeve of her puffer jacket and occasionally moans, rousing herself onto an elbow to take sips of water.

She keeps her eyes – her sick, reddened eyes – closed most of the time. I wonder if she sees me through their lids, sitting here at the edge of the bed, reading her words. I wonder if she sees me the way my dead husband saw me in Aix, when I stood beside his bed in the room smelling of olives. Sees me from inside herself.

In Aix, I left the room where his body lay and went outside. It was dusk. People stood about beneath the trees. I knew some of them but did not approach anyone. I did not cry or speak. My mouth was a barely discernible line that I could not have willed to move had I wanted it. It was the mouth from the portraits, the mouth of my own mute past.

I slipped through the gate and passed trees and stones and grass and a field of lavender. I came to a stream, running quiet and deep, and thought of throwing myself in, sinking without protest into the depths. I walked on, passing some cows in a field, watching the outline of their bodies against the sky, and it comforted me, a little, to know that they did not feel as I felt.

The hotel room is a mess. If I could, I'd sort her clothes into clean and dirty; I'd stack the dirty dishes and leave them outside the door for the staff to collect; I'd gather the books scattered across the floor and arrange them into neat piles. I'd try to help.

Though 'try' is perhaps the wrong word.

Once, in our living room, I joined in a conversation about art with my husband and his friends. I spoke about a painting that we had all seen in a gallery that day. I do not recall which painting now, nor do I recall what I said, but I remember that my voice took on a strange note; it seemed to be flung high and far from me, as if it were not my own. After I spoke the room turned quiet.

Somewhere a clock ticked. And then my husband said, 'Hortense, don't try.'

I went to our bedroom, taking the pins from my hair and letting it fall loose, my scalp aching, as it did night after night during the periods when I sat for the portraits. In only two of the portraits is my hair left loose. The first was done in the early days of our relationship, the second much later; I remember it well. It was the closest, in our later years, that my husband and I came to loving one another. One morning, as he was beginning his work, he stepped away from the canvas and across to where I sat, and with his long pale fingers began to arrange my hair. 'I have a brush,' I said, about to get up, but he murmured, 'No,' and went on moving the strands of hair, this way, that way, as if each had its own life.

I lay on the cold sheet and watched the strip of light that came under the door from the room where my husband and his friends still sat. In the murmur of their voices I listened for my name – not my real name but my nickname, La Boule – but I did not hear it; perhaps they didn't dare use that name in front of my husband. I had overheard it numerous times as I'd passed by a doorway or through a passageway, unseen. I did not like the name. But when I was upset, I drew an odd pleasure from dwelling on it, as if hidden in its shape existed some wonder that those who uttered it could not know.

Georgia's mother sits at the kitchen table writing what she'll say at the funeral. Ingrid and the girls are in the side room reading. The brothers are outside being brothers.

'I don't want others speaking for me. I want to speak for myself,' her mother says as she writes, her head tilted to the side as if this allows the words to slide out.

Georgia sweeps the floor with a worn straw broom. It scrapes across the floorboards and leaves the finer grains of dirt exactly where they were.

'You need a new broom,' she says.

'I like the old one,' her mother says.

Georgia takes the chairs out from around the table.

Her mother sniffs. Whatever she is writing is making her cry.

'There's nothing worse than a long funeral – long in the church, I mean.' She puts down the pen and looks out the window as she wipes her eyes with a hanky. The light makes streaks on her face. 'People just want to get outside the church and see one another, and *talk*. I've asked the priest to keep it short, and he should have no trouble. He never even met your father. He's not long come over from Vietnam. Australian priests are hard to come by, so they have to bring them in. Did you know that?'

'No, I didn't.' Georgia bends and manoeuvres the broom beneath the table. She avoids her mother's feet.

From outside comes the rhythmic thud of hooves and the barking of dogs. The brothers are mustering. Her father's dogs are skinny and eager, though fearful. They are working dogs, not pets. Her father was proud of the fact that not a single one had ever dared enter the house. You had to keep a bit of wild in a dog, he used to say, though not so much that they couldn't be trusted – the way a dingo couldn't be.

A dog then, like a daughter, had to walk a narrow path.

'Australian boys don't want to be priests anymore, it seems – and who can blame them?' her mother goes on. 'Such an odd life. In my grandparents' time, Catholic families expected that at least one son or daughter would go to the church. They used to call it "having one for the church". It's hard to believe now that people thought like that.'

Georgia arranges the chairs back around the table, keeping each chair level and placing them carefully, just so, as if they are vessels in danger of spilling.

'I don't know. This family thought like that,' she says.

Her mother gives her a hard look that is also a wounded look. Her mother is skilful at looks. 'You always twist things,' she says.

Georgia and Ingrid walk along a cattle track next to the creek. The girls run ahead. Zoe runs unevenly, with flailing arms, while Alice moves with long, effortless strides.

As Georgia and Ingrid walk, they look down at the pitted track, and at the long yellow grass on either side, and at the casuarinas in the dry creek bed that hiss when the wind blows through them.

'Remember one of the brothers found a stone axe around here?' Ingrid says, looking into the long grass beside the track. 'We took it to school to show the teacher.'

Georgia remembers holding the axe in the palm of her hand, the cool weight of it. She remembers running her fingers over its smooth sides and its worn, blunt blade. She remembers holding it out to the teacher, and the teacher taking it, saying, 'This needs to stay in a safe place.' Georgia doesn't know where that safe place was, or if the axe is still there.

The land is brushed with the shadows of trees and rocks and the crooked fences that divide the paddocks; it is brushed with the shadows of clouds and ridges and the hills themselves. Everything casts a shadow. There are brothers dotted here and there, some on horseback, others on foot. One chops at a tree with an axe; another uncoils barbed wire to string a fence; another, from his seat on a horse, admonishes a dog for chasing cattle. They all wear wide-brimmed felt hats like their father wore. They nod at Ingrid and Georgia as they pass and then get on with their work, busy inside the fairytale they grew up in here on the farm.

Years later Georgia will come to know this is the land of the Yuggera people, but for now, in 1990, although aware that this is stolen land, she doesn't know the name of the people that it really belongs to, the people who made the stone axe, the axe that is supposedly in a 'safe place'. She knows that her great-grandfather signed a piece of paper that said the land was his, purchased from the Crown. Being Irish Catholic, he had always despised the Crown and the things that were done in Ireland in its name. But despising a thing didn't mean you couldn't do business with it.

The light begins to shift and fade, and the shadows grow long. She and Ingrid turn and retrace their steps along the cattle track to the house, the children again running ahead. They pass the brothers, who go on working till the last of the light, for that is part of the fairytale, sun-up to sundown. When they near the house, Georgia is suddenly alone near the woodheap, standing in the same spot she stood in twenty years earlier at this same time of day – dusk, when all things seem possible – when she saw Ingrid and the boy, the boy she would start to 'go with' in the weeks that followed. She can't remember, now, where it was that they went together – to the pictures? To a friend's house? To the café in the main street in town to eat fish and chips? But she remembers the feel of his skin, silky as the dusk here by the woodheap, and the space they squeezed their bodies into in the back of a car. She did not tell him about the baby; by the time she found out that she was pregnant they were no longer going together. The silky dusk is, after all, transient.

Ingrid and the girls have gone into the house, and she is alone at the woodheap, alone with the cold air wrapped around her, the chips of wood scattered on the ground – and now someone is beside her.

A brother. There he is. In his hat and work clothes, tall and muscular. The brothers are all stereotypes.

He must have been chopping wood, she thinks, noticing the axe cast aside against a log, its blade glinting in the dying light.

He takes off his hat, wipes his brow and smiles. 'Georgia,' he says, and she likes that he knows her name, the name that is not her name, the name that she lives by here on the page.

'You should have said something.' She cannot help but repeat the refrain.

His gaze narrows. 'What are you talking about?'

'You know what I'm talking about.'

'Oh, that.'

'Yes, that.'

'Nobody else said anything, so why would I?' His voice is light as air, and she wonders if he is actually here, standing beside her in the mounting dark, his eyes no longer bright; they have blended with the night.

And she remembers that long ago, she and this brother shared a love of books, that as children they sat side by side on the couch reading to one another, out loud and in turn, *Seven Little Australians*, a story that was part of the fairytale that formed her body, here on this farm, here on stolen land, here on land that, even now, despite all the evidence, she sometimes forgets really *was* stolen. For the thing that feels so wrong is that it doesn't feel wrong enough.

The brother leans forward and picks up the axe.

'What are you reading these days?' she asks – and right up to this day, in Paris, as she writes this story, she has never been sure of his answer to this question, for she knows that it contains some invention of her own.

'*The Poetics of Space*,' he answers in his airy voice. 'It's a philosophy book, a bit hard going. I don't know why I persist. But there's this line I keep returning to. "Shade, too, can be inhabited."'

'Shade.' She says the word as if she is holding it in her hand, as she once held the stone axe, feeling its temperature, its weight. 'Shade, as in, what is hidden?'

'I think so, yes.' He begins to move away towards the house, and she is aware of the unlikelihood that this wood-chopping, horseriding brother is in fact reading such a book, let alone that he keeps returning to the line: 'Shade, too, can be inhabited.' But years later, as she writes in a hotel in Paris with the book *The Poetics of Space* by her side, it does become likely.

No, it becomes more than likely; it becomes inevitable. This is how life enters a story, and a story enters life.

'Mum says you're overdoing the wood,' she calls after him. 'It's a bloody furnace in there. I risked my life just to stir a stew.'

He turns to her and laughs softly. 'When I come home, I revert to old habits. We all do. Even you.'

Tonight, she is more settled. Her chest rises and falls gently as she sleeps. There is even the twitch of a smile on her lips. *Rebecca is right*, I think. *She will get through this.* Beside the bed, near some dirty tissues, lies the book *The Poetics of Space.* I watch her face and think of her baby boy, who is now a man, and I hope that in the story she will get to meet him again. I hope that she will, and I'm sure that she won't. I open the laptop and read slowly, a little bit at a time. I make it last; I do not want the story to end.

Georgia and her mother lie on the bed. Georgia doesn't know where Ingrid is, nor Zoe and Alice, nor her brothers. And she doesn't care to know. This is a pause in the march of time towards her father's funeral, a pause in which she has her mother all to herself, with no other players waiting to come onstage – a pause in which something might happen.

The iron roof creaks. The bedroom window is white with the day that cannot come in, the day that is outside, the day that is just any old day – while here, inside, in the grey interior of her parents' bedroom, it is *this* day, four days after Georgia's father died.

Georgia lies beside her mother, watching her smooth nose pointing up at the pressed-metal ceiling. She can smell her mother, a smell that is barely there, but unmistakable: a smell Georgia knew before she knew herself.

They have just folded the washing together – it was piled here on the bed – and put all the clothes away in the cupboards and drawers. Her mother picked up each item that belonged to her husband as if it were a miracle, saying things like, 'His blue shirt. Will you look at that.'

'I'm exhausted,' her mother says now.

'It's grief,' Georgia says.

'I suppose it is.'

They lie there, the silence as thin as the light.

'You know, the other day he told me that he had an *epithany*,' her mother says.

'An *epithany*? Oh god,' Georgia says, and starts to laugh.

Her father sometimes used words that did not come naturally to him, words that his mind or his tongue would baulk at so that he mispronounced them. *Epithany*.

Her mother is laughing too. Beneath them the bed shakes. The flowers on the pressed-metal ceiling shake.

They gasp for breath. Through the window the bright any-old day looks in. Georgia tries to speak. There is a weight on her chest.

'Wh … wh …' Finally, she gets it out. 'What was the *epithany?*'

Her mother gives a long snort. 'I don't actually remember,' she says, which sets them off again.

Finally, they are quiet, the sun watchful at the window.

Georgia takes a breath; her heart beats against it. 'You should have said something.'

Her mother lies perfectly still, which tells Georgia that her mother knows exactly which 'something' she is talking about. A stone would be more responsive, Georgia thinks, though she knows that this stillness is more pronounced because it comes after the laughter. Everything is in relation, nothing on its own. No stone. No mother.

Her mother raises herself onto an elbow now, and the bed sways. The loose skin of her face gathers at the edge of her neck. She stands and smooths her hair and walks towards the door. 'Are you going to wallow in here all day?' she says, without looking back.

That night, after the washing up, Georgia goes to her room, the room from long ago. She lies down on the narrow bed she slept in as a child. Its springs creak. And her mind goes over the script that it knows by heart. *My mother does not believe in the pain of her own child. There is a wall in her when it comes to that pain. Why else would she use the word* wallow? It's a script that eventually bores her. She rolls over, flinging her arms out from the covers, feeling the cold air that comes in through the cracks between the silky oak boards. The house has never been airtight; it is a breathing house.

She hears the scurry of mice in the ceiling: the same mice, for all Georgia knows, from long ago. The past shifts towards the present, the present towards the past. This has been happening ever since Malcolm came to the café and told her the news about her father; everything began to shift then, and has been shifting in increments ever since.

Although that isn't quite true, is it? *Everything* began before that.

Four months earlier, Malcolm told her that he wanted a child. He'd told her this same thing years before, when they met and fell in love, and she'd let him know then that she didn't want children. He'd been okay with it, or so she'd thought. But he'd brought it up again four months ago, and she'd realised that, all along, he'd been hoping, or assuming, that she would change her mind. In this he was like her mother. *There's still time.* From her mother, it was predictable, but from Malcolm, it gave her a sense of betrayal so deep that she'd packed her bags and left him that same day. She'd stayed at a friend's place for a week before renting a flat in Arcadia Street near the beach and setting about putting her love for him in the past.

But the past has its own curiosity. She knows this. It leans into the present, craning its neck.

She lies there looking around her darkened childhood bedroom at the amorphous details of its furniture, details that will become sharpened and specific in daylight – the rusted lock on the wardrobe that never had a key, the chipped laminex top on the dresser, the bevelled edge of the mirror – and as she moves towards sleep, the conversation with her mother, even the word *wallow*, is softened, almost obliterated.

Her gaze comes to rest on a deeper darkness on top of the dresser. She blinks and takes a moment to know what it is. When she does a fury rises in her.

She springs out of bed and takes the shawl in both hands. It's prickly, cloying. She goes to the window and shoves it open, its old paint rasping, and hurls the shawl outside, hurls it so hard that her spine shudders. It flails in the glassy air, like a thing scared for its safety, a helpless thing.

Malcolm calls. She stands at the little phone table in the hallway. Light comes in the front door, inching across the polished floor.

His tone is clipped yet measured, like he's holding something back, and she realises it matches her own. It's as if, like the light, they can each only move at an infinitesimal pace.

'I'd like to come to the funeral, if it's alright with you.'

'Of course it's alright.'

'Your mother asked me to help carry the coffin.'

She gives a short laugh. 'As if there aren't enough brothers to do it.'

'I don't know why she asked me.'

'I know why.'

'I won't do it if you don't want me to.'

'Do what you like.'

Later she goes to her mother, who sits in the kitchen doing the last bit of hand sewing on the red dress.

'Malcolm and I are getting divorced, you know.'

Her mother looks up, pausing the movement of the needle. It glints in her hand. 'Don't do anything you might regret.'

'Have *you* done anything you might regret?'

'There you go, again.'

The morning of the funeral, Georgia stands in the front yard with Ingrid. One of the brothers is backing the car out of the garage. Ingrid wears stockings and heels and lipstick. Georgia remembers how her sister's mouth had looked as she slept when they were children, her lips slightly parted as if she were about to speak. Ingrid had often known the right thing to say, even if it was strange. Once, when Georgia had asthma in the night, Ingrid held her close in the narrow bed, and Georgia felt her sister's heart beating against hers. Ingrid had whispered to her, 'I am breathing for you, you know.'

'Do you still have the box?' Ingrid says now.

'What box?' Georgia says.

Her sister's eyes are shards of glass. In the sun they look almost soft. 'You know what box.'

Georgia shrugs. 'There are a lot of boxes in a person's life. A little specificity might help.'

'You know what box.'

The car appears out of the garage, sleek in the sun, just as Georgia hears the cry of a crow. She turns. There it is, in the silky oak, the saddest of birds, with its cracked, carefully modulated cry that is like a grief spread over years, a grief spread over decades, a grief that passes, almost, for ordinary life.

'Of course I have it.'

She wakes coughing again. Her eyes are bloodshot; she coughs so much she vomits over the side of the bed. Staggering, she makes her way to the bathroom, fills a cup with water, brings a towel, attempts to clean up, then flops back on the bed and starts to cry. Her breath is faint and raspy, and I imagine Ingrid holding her close when they were children, breathing for her. I wish I could do the same.

The family sits at the front of the church. Georgia beside her mother, Ingrid the other side. Someone plays an organ: sad, in a generic way.

And here come the brothers, carrying the coffin.

Now I can count them, Georgia thinks, but still, she cannot. They are uncountable in their dark suits with their sad faces and their careful steps; they multiply, contract.

The priest on the pulpit. He's from Vietnam, Georgia remembers. She studies him: thin with neatly combed hair; eyes bright behind glasses; hands that look, to Georgia, sinewy and toughened, like they have worked for a living, although she knows she is too far from him to be sure of this.

He speaks about Georgia's mother, saying that when he arrived in town some weeks earlier she made him feel so welcome. She cooked a meal for him and dropped it off at the presbytery. She was clearly a selfless person, a thoughtful person.

Beside her, her mother lowers her gaze to the floor. Praise embarrasses her while pleasing her. Tears drip off the end of her nose. Her shoulders shake. Georgia knows that a good daughter would reach out and put her arm around her mother about now – her mother who looks magnificent, it must be said, in her red velvet dress with its cowl neck that drapes elegantly across her shoulders and collarbones and makes her creamy skin look so soft. But Georgia does not put her arm around her mother. Because Georgia is not a good daughter. She is a daughter.

And now she is crying too, wiping her eyes with the back of her hand. The man in the coffin up at the altar, with its crown of flowers on top, is her father. The coffin's wood glows in a way wood is not supposed to glow, except when struck by lightning, perhaps. *A live tree split in two and glowing wet with rain; now that would be fit for a funeral*, she thinks. That would make the impossible real; that would cut through.

And now, as the priest talks on – she's no longer following what he's saying – she has a clear memory of her father carrying her on his shoulders when she was a little girl, his big hands holding her legs so that she would not fall, she holding on to his thick black hair, holding it tight, pulling at great tufts of it. It amazes her, now, that he did not complain about her pulling his hair, and she continues to cry, sobbing into the handkerchief her mother gave her in the car, and she is annoyed with herself for crying, for he is the same father who looked at the priest and said nothing.

But there they sit in her, these two images of her father, side by side. Everything in relation, nothing on its own. No stone. No father.

Her mother goes to the pulpit, her eyes bright, her chin up. She speaks about her husband in superlatives: he was *always* a good father, *always* a good husband, *always* a good farmer, *always* respected in the district. And though Georgia feels disdain for these generalisations, she recognises the man her mother is speaking about. It's not as if *always* is never true. It's that it wears thin. It's that it can't cover every situation, every deed. It's that *always* is seldom always.

Some of the mourners kneel, while others form two queues up the aisle for communion. Her mother goes first, the others deferring to her status as widow. The red dress falls beautifully from her hips. Georgia does not go to communion. She remains in the pew, kneeling on the padded board, and thinks of her father kneeling on the kitchen floor of the flat in Auchenflower, cleaning the grout between the tiles.

As a child she would come into the kitchen in the early morning and he would be kneeling at a chair, praying, although she didn't know what praying was then, and she's not sure she knows now. She remembers that once she asked him, 'Daddy, why are you kneeling there staring at that chair?' but he hadn't answered her, he'd gone right on with his staring. The fire had just been lit and she remembers the warmth of it spreading through the chilly kitchen, as through the window she watched the sunlight touching the trees on the very tip of the hill.

She realises now, as she watches her mother walk back from communion, looking solemnly at the floor, as if the floor is as good as a chair to stare at – she realises that that scene in the kitchen occupies a pivotal space in her. She is struck by the fact that it is linked, in her memory, to the image of her father kneeling on the floor of her flat a few years after her baby was born and taken from her, and that, in turn, it is linked to this scene she finds herself in now, kneeling in the church at her father's funeral.

Our lives are filled with emblems of loss, and they continue to reverberate in us, and sometimes, after years, they can bring us undone. This will happen to Georgia, years in the future, in Paris, as she watches two women kneel either side of their child in the street.

Communion is finished, and Georgia notices that people are sitting rather than kneeling. She puts her hands behind her on the seat and raises herself to sit. The priest is at the tabernacle, head bowed. She sits one side of her mother, Ingrid the other. Beyond Ingrid sit Zoe and Alice, who unobtrusively fidget and whisper to one another.

Georgia remembers sitting beside her father in the car as he drove her to the home for unmarried mothers. The sky was clear, with a few clouds on the horizon. Outside of town they stopped for petrol. The woman who worked the bowser told Georgia's father that rain was coming, and maybe hail; someone had just driven through from Dalby, she said, their car newly pockmarked.

'If it's hail, I hope it goes wide,' her father said, and the woman nodded. She put the petrol pump back in place and the two walked to the shop together for Georgia's father to pay, and Georgia watched from the car and noticed how tall and straight her father was as he walked, and how the woman, though the younger of the two, was slightly lopsided, as if from leaning to fill the cars with petrol. Georgia looked down at her own legs, in grey corduroy trousers, and through the window at the cars passing on the road and at the crops shining in the paddocks and at the sky with its far-off clouds, and then she opened the door and got out of the car and went around the back of the shop looking for a toilet. A grimy door, half open to the road. Inside it smelt of diesel. She rinsed her hands – there was no soap – and wiped them on her cords, and when she came back to the car her father was already inside with the motor running.

When they arrived in Brisbane he lifted her suitcase from the boot of the car, which he'd parked in a street lined with Moreton Bay figs, their shade so deep that Georgia could barely make out his face. He turned and said something to her, and there was a formality in his tone, as if he was shy, or nervous. The suitcase was between them – and she worried that she might not have packed everything she needed for her stay.

Now, years later, sitting at his funeral, she cannot remember what it was that he said to her, or if she said anything in reply.

The writer's face on the pillow is gaunt. As I watch it, I imagine a younger face, plump and unlined, as it was at her father's funeral. I imagine her mother sitting next to her in the church, wearing the red velvet dress.

And it occurs to me that although she wrote the story for Rebecca it is also for me, for there are certain details in common between her story and mine. It seems that she has left me clues.

For instance, there is the red velvet of her mother's dress. It is like the velvet of the chair in which I sat while my husband painted *Madame Cezanne in a Red Armchair*. I used to put my hand to that fabric whenever my husband turned away to mix more paint; it was slippery and soft, comfortable but treacherous, as if any moment I might slide from it and onto the floor. And there is the box that Ingrid asks Georgia about, as the two stand in the front yard on the morning of the funeral. It reminds me of my mother-in-law's little boxes containing the baby teeth of my husband and his sisters that I burnt in the fire. I remember pulling the charred boxes from the ashes and, looking inside, finding that the teeth were barely scorched. For days afterwards I carried the teeth around with me in the pocket of my dress, like charms. I could not decide if their presence made me feel better or worse. Then, one day, while walking beside the river, I reached into my pocket and threw them as far as I could. They made a scatter of tiny marks on the water before sinking forever.

And there is the little box that the writer took from the drawer in Bondi just weeks ago, the box she opened and looked into, but closed before I could see inside, saying: 'It's nothing to do with you.'

But if they are clues, where are they leading me, and for what purpose?

Outside the church Georgia sees a girl from school. The girl is now a woman. Which shouldn't be surprising; it's twenty years since school. Cherry Pickering. Georgia remembers the woman's name as the woman turns to her.

At school she was known as 'Cherry Picker', relatively benign as high school nicknames went. There was a teacher called Mr Strange. That had provided greater scope, especially when it was discovered that his first name was Richard.

Cherry Pickering comes up to her and says, 'I'm sorry about your dad.'

'Did you know him?' says Georgia, who can't for the moment think why Cherry would be here at her father's funeral.

'Of course I knew him. He used to come and get you from my house. Don't you remember? But I'm not here for him. I'm here for you.' She peers at Georgia, shyly urging her to remember, to confirm that Cherry's version of history is her version, too.

And it's coming back. No, it's not coming back, but coming into existence, that Cherry was not just a girl in her class, but her friend. Cherry was a town kid, and Georgia was a country kid. Georgia used to stay some weekends at Cherry's house, in Spencer Street up near the Catholic church. They'd go out to the pictures together, walking down Railway Street dressed in short tops that showed their midriffs, the dusty air against their tummies a song that sang itself to them and through them, a song of adolescence and coming of age, a song that led them straight to the back row of the picture theatre where they sat with boys and learnt to kiss by the caress of the air on their tummies as much as by putting their mouths against those of the boys.

'Hello,' Georgia says and gives Cherry a hug. 'I'm sorry to seem distant, I'm … It's strange to lose a parent.'

'I lost my mum last year,' Cherry says. 'I know what it's like.'

'Oh, I'm sorry.'

'It's okay.' Cherry cocks her head, looks down, and Georgia realises there is a child standing between them, a little girl of about four.

'Okay, sweetie, we'll visit Iris after this. I'm just talking to Georgia now. We used to go to school together.'

The child stares up at Georgia as if staring might make her go away.

'We lost touch,' Cherry says, turning back to Georgia.

'I went away to uni.'

'We lost touch before that.' Cherry gives a small smile. She has lovely teeth, and Georgia remembers these lovely teeth from years ago, and how a boy had once told Cherry that her teeth were as straight as his aunt's, and later Cherry found out that his aunt wore dentures, and yet the boy had genuinely meant it as a compliment, and Cherry and Georgia had laughed almost until they cried while lying on Cherry's bed with the poster of Jim Morrison above it, and Cherry, when she at last gained breath enough to speak, had pointed to the poster and said, 'When will we ever meet real boys, like that?'

'It was year eleven. You went away. One day you were here, the next you were gone. You never said anything. And then at the start of year twelve you were back.'

'Do you know where I went?' Georgia asks.

'Everyone knew.'

'You're not everyone.'

'Of course I knew.'

'You never said.'

'I waited for *you* to say. I ... I wish I'd known then what I know now.'

'What do you know now?'

The sunlight falls on the grass at their feet. It falls on Cherry's shoulders and Georgia's shoulders. A weight. Holding them.

'I know now that I should have said whatever words came into my mind. But I thought there must be better words, *right* words, grown-up words.'

'I'm bored,' Sweetie moans and runs furiously on the spot. She pulls at her mother's dress. 'I'm *so* bored.'

'Whereas this kid doesn't have that problem.' Cherry rests her hand on Sweetie's head.

'And may she never have it,' Georgia says.

'I won't come to the cemetery.' Cherry leans forward and kisses Georgia's cheek. 'I have to get going.'

People stand around outside the church talking, wiping tears, laughing. Georgia watches them; she is a part of it all, but separate. She exists in silence – her own, and the silence of others. And here come the brothers with the coffin, heading towards the hearse. Through the groups of people they walk, slow and careful, and the people part to let them through. Of course they do; this is a funeral. And she sees Malcolm with the brothers, carrying the coffin.

He does not look at her. He is looking at the ground and the legs of the brother in front of him so that he does not trip. They must walk as one. A caterpillar of brothers and a soon-to-be-ex-husband.

The wake takes place at the farmhouse. There are cakes and plates of sandwiches. It reminds Georgia of the dances in the local hall when she was a child. There is family, extended family, neighbours. On the verandah, children run, thundering back and forth. Inside, people hold teacups or cans of beer, or both.

An elderly woman sits in the kitchen. Georgia thinks she is a neighbour. There is something about the woman's mouth that she remembers from long ago. Children run in and out of the kitchen for cake, nibbling the icing off the top and leaving the cake itself in bruised lumps on the bench.

The old woman says to another woman, who is handing her a cup of tea, 'I wonder if that parcel arrived.'

'What parcel, Mum?' says the woman, pausing with the tea.

'The one from the blind dogs. Remember, I put in an order for some towels from the blind dogs.'

'Mum, you know the *dogs* aren't blind, don't you?'

'I certainly hope they're not,' the old woman says, taking the cup in knotted hands.

Malcolm comes towards Georgia holding two beers. 'Let's go outside,' he says.

Outside it's cold. With no moon, the darkness holds sway. The stars are magnificent in their detail. Georgia and Malcolm walk around the side of the house.

'How are you?' he says.

'Okay. How are you?'

'Okay.' They sip their beers. And walk. And sip. The garden is big, with dark swathes of bush and brighter patches of grass.

'I don't know what to say,' he says.

'How do you mean?'

'I mean, whatever I say will be wrong. And now is probably not the time to talk about it. I'm sorry.'

'No. We're both here. Let's talk.'

'Okay.' He takes a swig of his beer. And now, somewhere in the night, a dingo howls, and others join in, and Georgia remembers lying in bed as a child and hearing this howling. She used to think that each dingo had its own hill to stand on, that each dingo was a lone voice calling through the darkness. But recently she read somewhere that when they howl, dingoes stand close to one another.

'You can't wait your whole life for him to contact you,' Malcolm says.

'Who said I'm waiting?'

'You know you're waiting.'

'Well, he might. One day. He might contact me. A lot do.'

'And a lot don't.'

'Why are you being cruel?' She stops walking, and he stops, too, and she tries to see his eyes, and he notices this and moves closer. His eyes are still bright in the darkness.

'I'm living in the here and now,' he says.

'You want a baby, and I don't. That's the here and now,' she says, as the dingoes start their howling again, one, then another, and another.

'But it's not true, is it? You *do* want a baby. You told me.'

'I want the baby I had,' she says.

'The baby you had,' he says.

She searches for a mocking tone in his voice but finds none. 'Yes, the baby I had,' she says more loudly, the words precious in their repetition, and she thinks, *We are like the dingoes, calling to one another while standing close.* 'And that wanting will never go away. I've told you all this.'

'Yes, you've told me.' His voice is soft, and sad, and she wishes it was hard, and angry. It might be easier.

From the verandah the thunder of the children's feet. From inside the house the tinkle of glasses, voices, a whoop of laughter.

Now that she is standing still, the cold trickles over her head, across her shoulders, down her back. She begins to shiver.

'You should have a coat.'

'I don't want one.'

'I haven't stopped loving you.' His voice is so quiet that she edges closer still. She can smell the wool of his coat. 'I hoped I would. But I haven't.'

She goes to take a swig of her beer but hesitates, then says, 'Let's go in.'

But he's peering at something beyond her, and now he steps forward to where the light shines from a window. Her bedroom window – she can see the corner of the dresser inside. Just below the window, in the spindly branches of a shrub, some shadowy thing lies; it springs to him, or seems to in the half-dark.

'Here you go.' He steps back and puts the thing around her; it is slightly damp and soft.

And everything that did not happen but should have happened is there in the weight of it, in the shape of it across her shoulders, in the hang of it down her back; all of it there in the stitches, in the complicated pattern, in the one or two mistakes. And now his arms are open and she steps into them and warmth flows through her, warmth from him, and warmth from the damp shawl, because wool, she suddenly remembers her mother saying once, is a remarkable fibre in that even when it is wet it remains warm against the skin; and she is racked by great, shuddering sobs, and he goes on holding her until the children run out of energy and leave the verandah and the voices and laughter fade and doors close and cars drive off and the house is very quiet.

He stays the night, sleeping in one of the brothers' rooms. At breakfast, she doesn't look at his face, only at his hands as he butters toast. Later, he leaves for the airport, and Ingrid and the girls leave, and Georgia and her mother stand on the verandah, waving. The brothers leave too – the brothers who never really became known to her. Even the brother she spoke to at the woodheap, the brother who told her about the book *The Poetics of Space*, even that brother had been scarcely real to her, scarcely himself, his voice like a breeze in the casuarinas, his body inconclusive in the dark.

Shade, too, can be inhabited, writes the author of that book, and Georgia wonders now, years later, in a hotel in Paris, if such a thing is ever possible. To inhabit shade. For her son is a shadow. She cannot remember his face, but she has a sense of it, a sense that is difficult to describe – even, or especially, to herself. It is featureless, but it exists, missing but always there.

But he is more than shadow. He is weight. Bachelard, in the book, doesn't mention weight in relation to shade. At least, as she sits on the bed in Paris writing these words while outside the window an illness drifts, weightless, she cannot recall that he mentions it, and she has read the book several times over the years.

She cannot remember her son's face. But the weight of him has stayed with her. There it is as she picks up a grapefruit in Coles, as she collects a parcel at the post office, as she gathers armfuls of leaf litter from the garden to carry to the compost. In the supermarket, once, while holding a bag of avocados, she almost dropped to her knees and wailed because the bag was the *exact* weight of him; she was convinced.

Georgia remains at the farm with her mother for a couple more days, just the two of them. They go through her father's belongings. She helps her mother drag his clothes from the wardrobe and onto the bed. The winter things smell of camphor. Her mother makes a pile for this brother and a pile for that brother. They talk about each of the items of clothing, who will get what – those grey trousers, will such-and-such a brother wear them? 'If he doesn't, he can give them to Vinnies,' her mother says. Georgia thinks that most of the clothing will end up at Vinnies, and perhaps her mother thinks this too. But it's the act of making the piles, the act of assigning the items, that is important.

Her mother takes a hat from a drawer. It's still in its clear plastic wrapping. She lays it on the bed. 'I got him this Akubra for his birthday. He never got a chance to wear it.'

They both stand looking at the hat.

Her mother turns to her. 'Would it fit Malcolm, do you think?'

'I don't know.'

'Would you take it for him?'

'What makes you think I'll be seeing him? Besides, he has his own hat.'

'I suppose it's not a style he'd like.' Her mother tilts her head as if to see the hat anew.

'It's nothing to do with the style.'

'He never got a chance to wear it,' her mother says again, her shoulders slumping, as if here is the greatest part of the whole tragedy: an unworn hat.

The next morning, early, her mother drives her to the airport in Brisbane. They don't say much. The sun rises, slanting across the bare hills.

In Sydney the buildings are cramped and disgruntled; she always notices this after she's been to the farm. The taxi passes Coogee Beach, the sky overcast, the waves flat; there are not many people about. She remembers walking on the beach just before she heard the news about her father; she remembers the coldness of the sand, the glassy surface of the water, and how the sun rose and formed shadows.

It was then that she'd entered this story; it was then that she became Georgia, named after Georgia O'Keeffe, who ripped the pink satin lining from her unfaithful husband's coffin and re-sewed it in white linen, who destroyed and then reclaimed that tender space.

There are ways of being close to our most horrendous hurt and still being able to live.

Coming into her apartment she dumps her suitcase and goes to the phone.

'Malcolm.'

'Georgia.' His voice is warm but hesitant. He waits.

Through the window comes the sound of a woman singing. The song rises up through the gap between the buildings. Georgia can't make out the words, nor, even, the tune, but the song is familiar to her, and it is this sense of the familiar mixed with the unknown that she will remember later, whenever she thinks of this day.

'Come over,' she says.

PART III

THERE ARE NO MORE WORDS. I scroll on, but there is only the blank page.

It is early evening. The writer lies in deep shadow on the bed. From outside comes the sound of the traffic, the ever-present wail of ambulances, an occasional voice from the street, and from somewhere, near or far, the scream of cats.

Time inches forward. Without the story, how will I spend the long night?

I move closer to her. I can almost feel her breath on my cheek. Her face looks calm, her eyelids soft. I recall her grandson's sleeping face and that of my own son. The faces of the sleeping harbour the hopes of those who watch. The worst is over, I think. And now, almost against my will, for that is how such things begin, as if they create themselves, I start to tell her my story. I tell her the things that I did not tell her when she was writing the book about me, the things that mostly I have not thought of in a long while.

I start with childhood. Not because it happened first, but because childhood imbues itself in the whole of life; childhood is a long brushstroke.

I do not remember my childhood home, not clearly, I say to her, as she sleeps, her breath even and deep. It was somewhere in the country. There were fields all around. I loved the plants standing in rows; I cannot remember which plants, just that they stood in rows, and that the sun loved them. The sun was a thing that had feelings, back then.

Later, when I became a bookbinder in Paris, I thought about those fields with their rows of crops as I learnt to make stitches in paper, stitches to hold a story, stitches to hold a whole world.

I don't recall much about the house itself, but I remember the feeling of being in it: the smell of freshly dug potatoes, the feel of laughter in my body, the sense of satisfaction at my smooth and tidy dress, and the sounds of my parents and my younger sister moving through the rooms, going this way, that way, their footsteps firm with purpose. Everyone was busy in that house; there was washing, cooking, cleaning, bringing in the crops. My little sister helped me peel potatoes for the meal. Nobody sat around reading books or staring dreamily into space.

When I met my husband and saw that his day was composed of such things, I was at first surprised and after that a little envious. Sitting for my portrait was a novelty, and a welcome one. It offered me rest and the chance to stare dreamily into space. But I soon learnt that it is not possible to truly dream in stillness, that dreaming requires movement, no matter how small – a scratch of the chin, a shifting of the gaze, a turn of the head. But if I did any of these things my husband threw his arms in the air and screamed.

Sitting was a trap, then, that I mistook for freedom. My childhood was happy, as far as I can tell. But happiness, to a child, is finite. A child is not stupid. A child knows what adults pretend to forget – that in the corners of the happy home lives unhappiness, and that one day they will find it. All it takes is a little curiosity. They have simply to go to the corner of a room and stand staring at the right-angled meeting of walls.

It would be easy to claim that *he* made me unhappy, but the truth is I knew unhappiness before I met him; my sister died when I was seven, my mother when I was sixteen. My sister became ill not long before we moved to Paris. 'She's in heaven now,' my mother told me one morning, her voice smooth and impassive, and I knew that pain hid beneath that voice like a stone beneath the ground.

My mother was the strong one in her marriage, the one who worked hardest and saw the way forward, the one who said we should move to Paris, for instance, and who seemed to have little feeling in her; she was all work and decisions. My father turned quiet after my sister died, and when my mother died quieter still; when I spoke to him, he looked through me as if I wasn't there. Three years later I met my husband.

The hours, the weeks, the years spent sitting. It makes me breathless, now, to think of them. They were an odyssey for which I never packed a bag. An odyssey for which I never left my chair. An odyssey for which the sky through the window with its passing birds was the only measure of adventure I had.

Rebecca calls to say she has bought her mother a ticket home.

'You leave in ten days.'

'*Ten days*,' the writer croaks.

'You'll need that time to recover. And to be sure you're not still contagious.'

'I'll be bored silly in this room.'

'If you're bored it means you're getting better.' Rebecca sounds hopeful.

'I am getting better – although it goes up and down. It's a weird illness.'

'Do you have the energy to read?'

'Not yet.'

'What about watching a film?'

'I couldn't look at a screen for that long. I still can't … focus.'

'You'll get there. You're doing great.'

'Great is stretching it.'

'You *are*.'

'I'm finding it hard.

'I wish I could do more.'

'You're doing plenty.'

'I'm not.'

'You *are*.'

They both laugh softly, and then Rebecca says, 'Is Hortense still there?'

'Hortense?' The writer says my name almost as if it is new to her. 'I'm not sure. At least, I haven't thought of her in a while. Why?'

'I was thinking about her just this morning. I was wondering if you might finish that book.'

'Oh, I doubt it. I wrote something else, just before I got sick.'

'Yes, you told me. But, somehow, I can't believe she's gone. I mean, whenever you talked about her, she was so real.'

'It's not enough that a character is real. They need a world to be real in.'

'So, what's the other story about?'

'I can't talk about it.'

'But it's finished?'

'Almost. There's just the final chapter to write. I'll have to write it when I get home. Which is kind of apt, as it takes place in my house.'

'And you're happy with it so far?'

'Happy is not a word I'd use. But there's something satisfying about it.'

'A reader right now might be helpful, to give you an outside perspective. Like how Dad used to read for you.'

'You know, he was there with me when I first saw Hortense. When we were visiting you in Boston.'

'I remember you going to the gallery. I had to work that day, or I would have gone with you.'

'There was a couple having an argument, one of those awful, quiet arguments that seem so civil, but you sense they are devastating. They were standing right in front of *Madame Cezanne in a Red Armchair*. Thankfully, they left, and we were able to have a proper look. I was struck by the way Hortense sat in the chair, leaning a little to the side, almost as if she was about to stand. All it takes is some detail like that, some impression, to make you want to write a book.'

'You never told me that. And now you've abandoned the book and written something else.'

'I didn't abandon it. It's more that it just … led to something else.'

'Well, I'd be happy to read it.'

The writer pauses, takes a shallow breath, and when she speaks again her voice wobbles. I can't tell if she is on the verge of tears, or about to cough. 'That might be good.'

'Send it to me then,' Rebecca says.

'Alright. Just keep in mind that it's not quite finished. There's the final chapter to come.'

After the phone call, the writer pulls the laptop to her and types away for a short time, and then I hear the whoosh of an email being sent. Closing the laptop, she turns over in the bed.

So, Rebecca has the story, I think.

The dressmaker was my companion in my later years, I tell the writer, continuing my story that night. I do not remember her name. I am not good with names. At least, I am not good with them as I exist here, on the edge of your mind. You have stopped thinking about me; you told Rebecca this. Yet there remains a connection between us, I think. The mind is a map of compartments: some locked, others open a mere crack.

During the day I helped the dressmaker with her sewing. Sewing clothing and binding the pages of a book are not so different. Mostly I liked to do embroidery on the baby clothes she made and sold; on the collars of the christening gowns, I would create rows of little flowers and birds.

In the afternoon I'd begin to drink, and I'd put the sewing aside. I'd sit at the dressmaker's table with a bottle of wine and a glass. Sometimes the dressmaker joined me, but mostly she was busy with cooking, cleaning or washing. Sometimes her grandchildren visited, sometimes my own, all fat-cheeked and bright-eyed. Children are blameless until they grow up and become the blamed. I let them sit on my shin as I jigged one leg up and down and they hung on to my knee as if they were on a pony. Later, my legs were cramped with arthritis, and I could no longer give them rides, although by then they were past the age for such things.

One of the dressmaker's granddaughters died from the Spanish flu. I visited her on what turned out to be the last day of her life, to take her a bowl of soup. Even close to death her eyes were bright; I wonder if eyes grow brighter as life fades.

People say that drink is the root of evil, but that is unfair to drink. I'm not even sure that evil exists, at least not on its own; perhaps it is a distorted part of good, and that is why it is impossible to isolate or cast out.

One night the dressmaker sat with me and joined me in a drink as I picked the pins from a crack that ran along one edge of the table. There were always pins in that crack. No matter how many you picked out, there were always more to find. 'I think they copulate in there,' I said to the dressmaker once.

It was the first anniversary of her granddaughter's death. That morning she'd taken flowers to the girl's grave.

She held up her glass. 'To my little angel,' she said, and took a sip and looked about the room; she was always searching for some chore to draw her in, and I expected her to get up from the table and resume her work. But she stayed sitting, and now she said, 'He didn't get you.'

'Who?' I said, looking up, a pin in one hand, my drink in the other. She watched me out of her small eyes. She'd shrunk over the past year. I put the pin on the middle of the table along with the others I'd collected, their heads all facing inwards and forming a pleasing circular shape.

'Your husband.'

'How do you mean?'

'I mean, he didn't understand you. He couldn't even paint you properly. Your face was far prettier than in any of those portraits.'

'My face was never pretty.'

'It was prettier than *he* made it.'

'He wasn't interested in prettiness.'

'That was what was wrong with the man, right there.'

Later, as she helped me to the toilet, and then to bed, as she took off my clothes and helped me into my nightdress, a thin nightdress – it showed my knees, wobbly with flesh – I thought about what she'd said.

He didn't get you.

I lay down, and through the window I watched the spire of Notre-Dame, the spire that now, a century later, is missing. It was summer and the dusk was a beautiful shade of blue. I lay in a swoon of drunkenness as I watched that spire. The dressmaker lay down beside me. Sometimes we slept together. It was a comfort to us both to hold one another, to feel the warm contours of one another's flesh, to murmur to one another, to share the delicious drift towards sleep. Some nights we lay awake talking, as through the window the stars made their slow, bright way across the sky. I, in my drunken pleasure, loved those stars as I had loved no living thing.

I reached across and lay a hand upon the dressmaker's heart and felt its deep, regular beat, and I thought that it was a wonder it beat at all, a wonder it could bear to after what had happened to her granddaughter, but hearts go on; I'm not sure how. It doesn't take much to break a heart, but to kill a heart seems to take much more.

My husband had a fear of being touched. Perhaps it was the greatest of his fears. It came from a childhood incident in which, at school, a boy had pushed him down the stairs. He only ever touched me when we made love, and even then there was an evasiveness. He never touched my face, for instance; my face he left to itself. And he made it known that he did not want me to touch his face, either: did not want it cradled, or kissed, or held to my breast. We did not make love so much as mate, armless, like owls.

When he first painted me, I thought that in some way he was touching me with his brush, caressing me, and this made me almost happy. But then I discovered the constriction of stillness. I saw that the birds through the window could move in their happiness, but I could not.

I tell you these things about my life as you sleep in your shadowy bed, and as I speak some glimmer begins; perhaps it is the approach of the dawn, or a light switched on in a building outside. Whatever it is it draws me on.

He loved his mother. When she died, he kept her things in a room of their own. I did not have a room of my own. In every place we lived, I shared the rooms with him and our son. Even during our periods of living apart – usually him in Aix and me in Paris – I did not have a room of my own; I had a room from which he was absent.

One day as I sat for my husband and the birds flew by outside the window, I was reminded of the day of our wedding. As I'd made my way down the staircase of his parents' mansion to go to the carriage that would take us to the town hall, I'd caught a glimpse through a window of a flock of tiny birds alighting in the olive trees. At the ceremony there was the coldness of his mother's smile, and the way my new father-in-law turned away from me, and the fact that my mother was not there because she was dead, and my father was not there although he'd given his consent.

And somehow, remembering all of these things, together, including the flock of birds descending into the olive trees – for when, in this world, is beauty ever shut out entirely from pain? – remembering these things, together, made me decide that as soon as he finished painting me that day I would go to the room he'd set aside for his dead mother's possessions, and I would drag them to the courtyard and strike the match.

My husband once declared, famously, 'I paint a head like a door.' What he meant, according to those who know about these things, was that he brought the same level of attention, and importance, the same level of *feeling*, to a door as he did to a head. In *Madame Cezanne in a Red Armchair*, for instance, the inanimate objects – the chair, the wallpaper, my high-necked blouse and striped skirt – have as much importance as my face and hands. Over the many sittings for that painting and others, I got to know something about inanimate objects: they keep to themselves. He interrogated them with his gaze, just as he interrogated me, but they gave nothing in return. They blinked back at him, unmoved. And yet, as I sat among them, they seemed to know about me, just as the stringed instruments in the music shop in front of the bookbinders had seemed to know as much about my life, about my secrets, about my future as I did myself. And in sitting with them, I learnt from them. I learnt to hold myself back. I was given no privacy, and so I made my own. Each sitting, I withheld some aspect of myself. Perhaps he liked it that way; perhaps it was the very thing that kept him painting me, time after time. Though, as some have pointed out, it was convenient for him to paint me; I was readily available and did not need to be paid.

Each Hortense in the twenty-nine portraits is uniquely herself, different from all the others. And they are all different from me. He gave feeling to the parts of me that he was able to; I can only assume that each time he painted me his feelings shifted. Yet there is one feature that art historians have noted remains recognisably mine in each of the portraits – the line of my top lip. My mother used to call it my stubborn top lip, for I would hold it like that whenever I insisted on getting my own way.

As the dark of night closed in and my drunkenness waned, with my hand on the dressmaker's heart that beat deep as a sea, I whispered, 'I did not *let* myself be got.'

The spire. There it is through the window as I wake in the bed with the dressmaker – it reaches up to the sky, up to the pink morning light.

The spire that is now missing, the spire that fell in.

In the room near the burnt church the writer wakes, and looks a little better. She stands and stretches her hands above her head. There is colour in her cheeks. She makes her way to the bathroom, a tentative spring in her step.

I remember lighting the candle in Notre-Dame, the way it sputtered, the little drips of wax that fell on my fingers.

And now a face comes to mind – or starts to. It hovers, incomplete.

She comes back from the bathroom wiping her wet hands on her track pants and, passing a pile of dirty clothes beside the television, she notices her husband's hat sitting on top. She picks it up and stands there looking at it, turning it over in her hands, and now – it happens both fast and slow, and it is like watching the child being hit; there is the same sense of surprise and shock mixed with a terrible inevitability – she falls, hat in hand, onto the white carpet.

She lies there, arms spread. She must have let go of the hat as she fell, for now it lies a little way from her, upturned. Her legs look crumpled, I'm not sure why, and then I realise that she is pulling them up beneath her – or trying to. Perhaps it is an attempt to comfort herself, as she did when she lay on the bed after the child was run over, her knees up to her chest.

'What can I do?' I say, but she stares through me, and now the face is coming into focus, the face of the one for whom I lit the candle, long ago – but as quickly as it appears it is obliterated, and the face of another takes its place, the face that is now before me, the face I have studied these past days with a gaze as intense as any painter.

'It was for you,' I whisper. 'I lit it for you.'

I can't be sure that she hears me. Her eyes are strangely bright, like the eyes of the dressmaker's granddaughter, and I know, without a doubt, that she is dying, here in this room we have shared, here in this tender space.

Some impetus takes hold of me, some piecing together of her story and mine – and I know what I must do. I move to the crack in the window, to where the air breathes in and out.

I have never admitted this to myself, but the crack is something that I have been wary of ever since we came to this room; I have never let myself venture too close to it. When I went to the window alone I stood well away, and when I went there with the writer I made sure that she was between me and it, just as my husband had once made sure that I was between him and a dog.

Is she breathing? Her chest is still as wood. But I think she watches me; her gaze shifts as I move.

Up close the crack is a multitude of lines, each going off in its own direction; some end abruptly, others reach further than I thought possible, becoming frail as stardust as they disappear. I take a breath, or seem to, and push ahead.

In a moment I am through and out the other side, out in the cold air of Paris, the air of my past, and I am falling, the wind whipping at my hair and face and dragging my arms upwards. Below me are rooftops, and the brown river, and the broken back of the burnt church.

But as I fall the air grows thicker, warmer. There is an ocean to my right now, the sun glinting on its surface, the shadow of currents beneath. Below is a street lined with trees. I land softly and hear the cry of a cockatoo.

I make my way down the street; through the warm air I stride. There is not much time. She is dying, and I am on the edge of her mind.

Now someone is here beside me. Rebecca. She gives me a quick smile and we fall into step, striding along, hip to hip. Reaching the writer's house, we go in the gate and past the paperbarks in her garden. Rebecca pulls a key from her pocket and lets us in. Down the hallway we go, the light shining soft in the windows. At the door to the writer's bedroom, I pause, for here it is: the final chapter.

Sitting on the bed, side by side with Rebecca, I point to the cupboard. She leans down and opens it, just as the writer did on our last night in Sydney. She reaches her hand in and fumbles around. It comes out with nothing.

'Try again,' I say, and she goes deeper, moving her hand this way and that, until at last it comes out with the little box.

There it rests in her palm, with its smooth wooden sides and its tiny, glimmering hinges.

It's nothing to do with you, the writer said on that night, and perhaps, at the time, it was true.

Gently Rebecca lifts the lid. Our heads almost touch as we bow to look inside.

In the box lies a lock of hair.

We turn and look into one another's eyes, and hers are filled with tears, and we bow our heads, again, to gaze inside, as through the window comes the sound of the sea breathing in and out, in and out, as if its secrets are nothing, really, but the going forward of life.

Acknowledgements

My sincere appreciation to Varuna the National Writers' House for a generous fellowship that enabled me to work on this book. In addition, I spent several alumni weeks at Varuna over a number of years and I extend my thanks to my fellow resident writers for their insightful comments; in particular to Yves Rees for their observation regarding the child in the street, which led me to the discovery of the narrative's pivotal event.

Early on, Peter Bishop and Mary Cunnane gave generous, honest feedback for which I am hugely grateful.

Thanks to Martin Shaw for finding the perfect publisher for this book and providing wise counsel along the way. He's a champion of literary fiction and a visionary; I can't thank him enough.

Much gratitude to Aviva Tuffield and Margot Lloyd at UQP. Talented, respectful, strident and kind, it was a joy to work with them both.

On a more personal note, heartfelt thanks to my daughter, Sophia, her husband, Dom, and my granddaughter, Gia. I can't accurately trace the line from you all to and through this book, but I know it is there.

To my stepdaughter, Kirra. I realised only recently that watching you paint and hearing you talk about your work helped me find the courage to write about art. My deepest thanks.

To my husband, Geoff. You were with me when I first saw Hortense in Paris in 2017, and you've been by my side through every stage of this book. My deepest gratitude for your unflagging support and faith.

To Mette Jakobsen, friend and fellow writer, thanks for your feedback on the manuscript and, as always, for our sustaining conversations.

To Jenny Fisher, thanks for reading an early beginning and telling me the truth.

To my brothers and sisters and extended family. Not one of you is in this book; its events and characters are invented. Yet our shared past was with me as I wrote. Thank you for your understanding.

I relied on several works to research this novel, notably: *The Poetics of Space* by Gaston Bachelard, *Madame Cezanne* by Dita Amory, *Hidden in the Shadow of the Master: The model-wives of Cezanne, Monet and Rodin* by Ruth Butler, *Cezanne* by Alex Danchev, *The Question of Painting* by Jorella Andrews, *Cezanne's Other* by Susan Sidlauskas, *Funny Weather: Art in an emergency* by Olivia Laing, the *Anthologia* blog's collection of Rilke's letters on Cezanne's paintings, 'Madame Cezanne and "The Truth in Painting"' by Erin Courtney Devine on the *New York Arts* website, the Museum of Fine Arts Boston website's entry on *Madame Cezanne in a Red Armchair*, and the Cleveland Museum of Art website's entry on *Mount Sainte-Victoire*.

Finally, I'd like to acknowledge and thank the Gadigal people of the Eora Nation on whose unceded land this book was written.

Joan C. Bell Prize

Angela O'Keefe's *The Sitter* is the 2024 recipient of the Joan C. Bell Prize from Zerogram Press. Our $10,000 prize is intended to reward inventive and innovative writing that continues and extends the tradition of innovative novels that enthrall the reader. The prize is named in honor of one of the great computer scientists in the early history of computing. Among a great many other accomplishments, Joan C. Bell co-designed the packet structure that made the Internet scalable to billions of devices, and if the history of the Internet were properly written, she would be considered one of the Mothers of the Internet. We honor her memory with our prize.